MW01688230

THE WETA SHED

by Brian Mossman

A broken promise
A betrayal of trust
A break of many years

... but then an unexpected opportunity, and a chance for a previously abused child to plan his revenge.

First published in
New Zealand in 2003 by
NATIONAL PACIFIC PRESS
PO Box 57-202
Mana 6230
Porirua, New Zealand
Ph 64 4 233 8204
E-mail: books@npp.co.nz

Copyright © Brian Mossman, 2003

This book is copyright under New Zealand law and the Berne Convention. All rights reserved. No part of this publication may be reproduced, stored in a retrieval system or transmitted in any form or by any means electronic, mechanical, photocopying, recording or otherwise, without the prior written permission of the publishers.

This is a work of fiction. Names, places, characters and incidents are either the product of the author's imagination or used fictitiously. Any resemblance to actual events, organisations or persons is entirely coincidental and beyond the intent of the author or publisher.

ISBN 0-9582448-4-7

Text artwork and page layout by Hutcheson, Bowman and Stewart, Wellington

Cover design by CAT Design

Printed by Hutcheson, Bowman and Stewart

To my wife Denise for her support

Brian Mossman was born in Auckland in 1949 and educated at eight schools as his father's employer progressively transferred the family south. Like many kids growing up through the 1950s and 1960s, Brian experienced a shift away from after-school activities such as building tree-huts and trolleys, and eeling in the Waikato, when the arrival of television drew everyone indoors. Nevertheless he looks back with fond memories on a childhood full of excitement and adventure, through a period many kids of today might have difficulty relating to.

A prearranged, but missed, instruction to read a book during the school holidays caught Brian on the hop during his Standard 4 year, and on the first day of the new term the overlooked book review was called for. Ever imaginative, he concocted a page of events and came up with a fictitious author for the book entitled "The Boy Who Ran Away". Oblivious to the deception, his teacher added glowing comments to the summary, and gave him a mark he was unable to match in any other subject during the rest of his education.

Some 40 years after manufacturing an article and having nothing to do one day, Brian sat down and started to write a fictional story using that earlier book review as its base. The sentences seemed to flow easily, and the end result was *The Weta Shed*.

Brian is happily married with successful grown-up daughters, and now lives in Auckland once again.

CHAPTER 1

The face stared back at him from the page. It was a wonder he recognised his Uncle Jim's photograph at all, but then how was he expected to? The guy was meant to have died an agonising death long ago. But here he was with that cruel, thin-lipped look of his. So much older after all these decades, yet such unmistakably familiar features. And still alive.

Bill Wilson could hardly contain himself. He wondered if anyone else was aware. Probably not. After all, the police gave up chasing Jim Dwyer many years ago. The loathing built inside him, and it was all he could do to stifle an outburst. He wanted to shout out, 'You bastard!' but it was hardly appropriate. Not here in front of everyone.

He tried to start on the article, but the picture kept his attention far longer than he cared for. With newspapers being such difficult things to read in confined spots, his impatience quickly showed as he folded uncooperative pages into a more manageable size so he could concentrate on the text. Passengers watching would have seen his annoyance from the outset. Everyone seemed to stare at one another, and while he had become used to this throughout the week, right now his thoughts were fully occupied and he was oblivious to any scrutiny. Above all, he could not get past the fact the old prick had successfully evaded everyone for so long, and if he gave the impression he was flustered, then there was good reason.

Bill had not been happy using an alternative form of transport these past few days, and now a mass of bad childhood memories added to his discomfort. With the paper as he wanted it, he quickly scanned the accompanying article. Just a simple item allowing those in, or nearing retirement, to express their views on the subject.

The day had started badly at 7.00 a.m. Weeks of drizzle followed by one day of fine, and then back to this again. He had expected the worst when delivering his car for gearbox repairs. These inconveniences usually went hand in hand with a turn in the weather. Only a light rain now after a sunny start, but nevertheless depressing. Days like this made any journey through crowded streets a real trial, and he thanked his lucky stars that the use of the bus service was a rarity for him. Fresh rain on a hot road was one of those smells he usually enjoyed, a warm and familiar aroma that did not hang around for too long. Just enough of a whiff to bring back pleasant memories of summer sun-showers here in New Zealand.

He had a few good memories of those days back in the 1950s and early 1960s. 'Only a few to partially off-set the bad,' he thought to himself. Anyway, the dusty scent of the road had done nothing for him today and the bus struggled on with a full load. 'A typical morning's crowd,' he thought. And a snooty lot as well, it seemed. They proceeded through peak-hour traffic at a steady pace, with just the engine noise and the odd clash of gears interrupting the silence. Bill knew he had little in common with any of the other passengers. They all seemed to be younger, business types for one thing. He certainly felt out of place on a bus, realising it was probably his uniform clashing with their suits. A case of him and them perhaps. In both instances, clothing that went with the job. It was as if all passengers sensed the difference, but on the other hand no one was really conversing anyway and so the semi-quiet continued.

His own fault, this temporary choice of transport. He was feeling disagreeable, and amongst other things the cost of car repairs had been playing on his mind. It was true he could have just as easily avoided all this by having a colleague pick him up in one of the cars, but for some reason or another he had not pursued that option. In any event it was only expected to be a one-day inconvenience. It had grown to three days so far.

He looked around at them, thinking what a boring lot they all were. Sitting in silence with heads turned away, each consumed with his or her own thoughts. There was probably no real need for conversation to kill the time anyway. It would be quick enough at under half an hour, with enough entertainment just watching passengers getting on and off. He was a great people-watcher. It was a crucial part of his life these days. The job and all that.

'I've finished with this,' a faceless voice announced, anticipating her stop.

'So they can speak after all,' Bill quietly murmured to himself. The woman had risen from beside him to squeeze past others in the aisle. They had made way for her ungraciously. Everything was an inconvenience today. You could see it everywhere.

'Thanks,' he mumbled after her, louder this time, and pleased for something to look at.

The conversation, brief though it had been, had startled him. Like most of the others, Bill had briefly slipped into his own little world, becoming unaware of the movements and sounds around him. The sections of discarded newspaper had become intermingled with one another, and he began to reorganise them before starting to read. He was a methodical type. Liked things just so, and in situations like this was prepared to spend time straightening out wrinkles in each and every page.

Someone else slipped into the vacant spot beside him, crowding his space. Withdrawing further into the corner as best he could, he tried to start a conversation.

'Awkward things, newspapers,' he said after a while. It had been an opener, but was also an apology for any inconvenience he was causing his new companion.

'I rarely travel by bus,' he continued. 'Car's being repaired. Damn inconvenient too, on days like this. Bill Wilson's the name by the way.'

It had been no use, and he let his attempt die there amongst the droning noises of the engine.

And that is basically how the morning unfolded. He had been sitting uncomfortably for ten minutes or so before making a start, first with the headlines, and then opening the paper somewhere in the middle. It had not been an immediate awareness, but something had made him dwell on the photo. A vague familiarity with the face that stared back at him, and then a sudden unmistakable recognition, like seeing a ghost from his past. He had stared long and hard, then closed the pages. When looking again, a moment or so later, he still found it hard to accept that Jim Dwyer was alive.

'God, he's aged,' he muttered quietly to himself. And in a quivering voice, 'How on earth did you survive the fire?'

The bus trip continued. Nearly over. Just a few more stops. Glancing down he was again caught unawares. The picture was almost taunting him now, until he fixed the situation by turning that section of the paper face down on his lap. He was having difficulty coping with the shock, the disbelief, and the sheer hatred he felt for the guy. Bill did his best, for the moment, to get the article out of his mind by turning his attention to the others. There were those struggling to cope with a swaying bus. Mad rush to catch it at the last minute, then that pained look of dismay and indignation at the inconvenience of having to stand. Others openly displayed their disapproval at the turn in the weather, staring mindlessly at fogged-up windows. No one seemed prepared to dirty themselves by wiping clear the steamed-up glass for a better view. An abhorrence for the smell of wet raincoats showed in one or two expressions.

'An impatient lot,' he thought, thinking nothing of it as he cleared the window with his own cuff. At least he was prepared to do something to ensure he knew the cause for their delay. Some minor traffic congestion, but the bus had not been held up for very long, and the steady motion when it restarted, together with the weather outside, made it easy for most passengers to relax. Not Bill Wilson though. He was on edge.

'Rain's stopped,' a passenger somewhere up front announced loudly. There was a general murmur of approval. But for one passenger the comment was not enough to brighten his day.

• • • • • • •

Weeks became months, and the delay did not help the situation. Bill thought of Jim Dwyer daily. Sitting in the park on a day off would have been a pleasure on any other occasion. But today was different. Today he was here for a specific purpose, and he wondered how he would cope with the impending confrontation.

A silver shape flashed overhead, disturbing his thoughts. Overhanging branches obstructed his view, allowing only a fleeting glimpse. The angle was wrong so he was unable to make out the airline, but it hardly mattered. 'Lucky buggers', he thought. Probably heading for Singapore or LA. Or any of those many other places he would never get to visit.

'Oh to have money to travel,' he imagined.

The noise seemed to intensify as it passed, and the plane soon climbed out of sight losing itself amongst the clouds. Quiet was restored, and except for the dull background sound of the city there was nothing to listen to. All Bill could do was wait.

He had been doing a lot of thinking lately, and those shrieking engines had caused his thoughts to linger on an incident that had happened many years earlier. An incident in fact linked with the reason he was waiting here today. It helped him pass the time. Remembering, but also imagining, things that may have happened. Wreckage in the bush. Torn fuselage. Pieces of metal violently strewn about. Finer details long forgotten, and some facts never known in the first place. Just guessing really.

It had probably been during that decade leading up to the war, he calculated. Bill had no idea when aerial top-dressing of fertiliser had started in New Zealand. He knew over time they had used all types of carriers to spread the stuff over farmland. Best effect had been from the air, but there had been casualties in those early days, and some fatalities too. May not have even been a top-dresser. Who would know? He had seen the remains, though, but many years after the event.

So here he was today, waiting and watching and thinking back. It had been a long time coming. Sure, there had been many sunny times in his life. But there had been grey times too. Like today for instance. Nothing to do with the weather. In fact, if he could keep his mind off the matter at hand it was rather pleasant sitting in the park alone. Well it had been, briefly. A derelict joined him, and Bill generously let him loudly air his knowledge about whatever subject it was he was going on about. He could just as easily have shooed him away.

'These slatted park benches are the same as those varnished seats we had in the trams you know.'

The tram-cars the 'dero' referred to were those that had plied the streets of Auckland some thirty years earlier.

'This one's been covered with everyone's initials,' he said tracing a grubby finger over some of the letters. Sanding the slats had failed to erase all scratches in the woodwork completely, but fresh paint in recent weeks had filled and partially obliterated most of the handiwork of earlier generations. A few of the words remained legible and made interesting reading. Most of the script was dirty though. The dero deliberately drew attention to a carved sentence or two and laughed at the crude message. His body aroma was so bad, however, that Bill was relieved when the man eventually shuffled off down the path to investigate council rubbish bins. Bins that possibly represented his main source of daily rationing. A number of older 'down and outs' lived in this area. Lived the rough life and seemed none the worse for it. Bill hoped he would never get to that stage.

He had been doing his best to relax before the interruption, but now found it impossible to revert to his earlier level of calm. His gut feeling was that the meeting he had half-planned would happen this morning. He hoped it would, and yet in a way he dreaded the outcome. He tried to concentrate on more pleasant things. Spring flowers were emerging for one thing. Council gardeners had carefully planted these in clumps at the base of each mature tree. Daffodils and jonquils. They bobbed and danced their colourful heads in the breeze, moving in time with the mass of branches that now had that slight hint of green. There was just enough of a chill this morning to remind him that winter had barely finished. The majestic boughs of larger trees culminated above him in a tangle of smaller branches. He gazed up, thinking that some of these must have dated back to the turn of the previous century. Sunlight filtered through and a few new leaves declared the change of seasons.

Bill opened his wallet and removed something. He took his time carefully unfolding the paper which had yellowed with age, and had begun to tear along its creases from past use. It was a letter written to him years ago, and one he had read and re-read on many occasions since.

My dearest William and Kitty,

By the time you are old enough to read this letter yourselves, the war will be over. God willing, peace will have been restored. Be strong both of you, for the future will present you with countless opportunities ....

It went on, naturally, but he read no further. He knew the words by heart. A letter his parents had sent with him as a child in an envelope pinned to his jacket. Bill Wilson sat calmly in the peace and quiet. Above all else these days he lived for the quiet. There was no pressure in his job. He often had time off as a result of accumulated leave. His street was one of those dead end ones with limited parking. He was lucky in that respect. Few of the residents seemed to have cars, and he hardly ever saw them coming and going. It was a quiet area, and that had been part of the initial attraction when selecting a house to rent. That, and the fact that it felt good and comfortable. Just two bedrooms. No one sharing with him. He preferred it that way. He was hardly unsociable. Quite the opposite. Well no, he had to acknowledge, he was pretty anti-social. He had never had a party for example. How does one start to organise such a thing? Who would come? Not work mates. His relationship with colleagues was not that strong. And then there was that bit of an age difference at work as well.

Bill had not progressed in his particular organisation as others had. He had not married, and perhaps that had had some effect on his career chances. Those who got places had all been married. It was easier for them to entertain he assumed, and those moving in the same circles recreationally seemed to enhance their promotional chances. He liked people, but if he was truthful about it he was also a bit of a loner. The house he occupied suited a loner. He had lived in the general area for ages, moving about from time to time. He had found this one some months ago. Seen its potential. Kicked the garden into shape. A few new pieces of furniture. Bit of a paint-up in the kitchen. The rent was reasonable, and there had been no further contact with the landlord since moving in. He paid on time and it was left at that. It was an arrangement that suited him well.

It did not take long before the local streets were no longer strangers to him. In fact, he was familiar with them all now. The result of taking a different route each day in an effort to keep fit by walking. Both were requirements of the job. Local knowledge and fitness. Despite the miles he was prepared to put in, his appreciation for food had had an adverse effect. One had not quite countered the other. The extra weight was inevitable. Not the 'thin kid' of years ago.

Stumbling across this particular public reserve by accident had been a bonus. A small patch of bush and planted grasses with a short meandering walkway. Sure there were old trees from the home country, but a lot of it had been planted out in native foliage. And judging by the number he had seen in here, few of the busy inner city working residents knew of its existence. Since finding it, he had treated the park as his own little bit of paradise. He loved the bush, and did not regard this mixture of trees from other countries as being in any way out of place with the evergreen foliage of the natives. In fact, it was a rather sympathetic mix of oak, lancewood and totara.

Bill's thoughts reverted from the pleasantness of the day to the real reason he was here this morning, and he searched the road now in both directions as far as he could see. It was probably too early to expect many locals to be up and about. That did not matter though. He simply wanted to be prepared. In any event it suited him today not to have to pass the obligatory 'good morning' to all and sundry. All he wanted was to sit alone, especially after his earlier experience with an unwashed dero.

There was only one person in particular he was waiting for. While many years had passed, he envisaged no difficulty in recognising his quarry. It was a process of setting a trap that needed to be followed meticulously, and this stage would represent his first step in the exercise. Perhaps he would relax a little once the initial part of his plan was successfully behind him. A bit of activity in the street at last, but only a couple of kids. Bill gave them no further attention, leaned back, made himself comfortable again, and sat fingering the deep scars in the seat. Once more his thoughts drifted, and he became preoccupied for a moment with his own scars. There were things that needed doing. And things that simply had to be done. But it was knowing where to start that worried him.

September 1990. Where had the years gone? It would be his forty-seventh birthday this time around. Born in 1943. Seemed so long ago, and of course it was. Looking back he saw a life with nothing much to show for it until these more recent years. Most guys his age would have had grown up children by now and a home and other comforts. For his part, he had little in the way of tangible assets. There had been no consistency in his work or income for many of those years, and a long-term interest in the horses a while back had taken its toll until he had brought that problem under control.

He continued reminiscing, his mind full of hurtful memories and thoughts of unfinished business. His step-father... well Jim was not really... actually he was only a distant relative. Just someone who had stepped in to help and who had stayed on too long. Jim Dwyer had been off the scene now for many years. Killed in a fire, or so everyone had understood. Then the name and photo had come up in a newspaper article on retired folk and that had shaken him. He still thought of that day. Almost three months back since the bus trip. Would have missed it altogether had the paper not been thrust into his hands by a fellow passenger. Interviews with randomly selected elderly 'locals'. Just another of many newspaper articles during 1990 on the country's elderly. It had stirred his memories and emotions. It was him all right. Jim Dwyer. And after all this time, living only a matter of kilometres from him. What a hideous turn-up that had been. Bill had banished him from his thoughts after certain events in the 1950s, and to all intents and purposes had tried to start his life afresh. That was a joke. Some life. But here he was four decades on, having tracked him down. Waiting to confront the old prick with the words... 'Hey! Bastard! Remember me?'

He intended spitting the words out. They would be backed by forty-odd years of bitterness and hatred. And he was determined to make it show.

CHAPTER 2

In 1944 kids had no real idea of what was going on. It was a time of turmoil and loss. The fighting raged on and frequent bombings became normal fare. Here in England everyone felt the war would last forever. Most realised it was the nation's elderly and young who would suffer the most, and with this in mind the government arranged for all kinds of people to be evacuated. But particularly children.

William (no one called him Bill at that time) and his sister Kitty were amongst a crush of people on the platform. The train had been late in arriving, and now the crowd moved forward as a mass, with everyone eager to escape to some measure of safety outside the city limits. They had had their share of destruction and carnage. Had seen the raw effect of bombing and smelled the unforgettable dusty aroma of pulverised concrete hanging for ages in the air.

Air raid sirens wailed yet again, and while the crowd showed signs of agitation no one was prepared to seek shelter and risk losing their place. A nurse carried William on board. He was about a year old and still in nappies. Parents stood back and waved their goodbyes, having been assured their kids were the fortunate ones. They were told that protection would come from caring country folk who were opening their homes and hearts to a nation in need. With a rush of steam there was forward movement at last, and the carriages crept away from the cheering but tearful throng. It had been an epic undertaking organising this vast army of youngsters. The mass exodus left a strange silence in the streets of most cities and many towns. They headed, as had many before them, to unknown destinations.

William was to be told all about this, years later. He learned too that his parents had something to do with essential services. That was why it had been necessary for them to stay behind. Some of the kids in their carriage were less than ideal travelling companions. They brought with them the smells and habits associated with the slums and back streets of places like Birmingham. Tired and hungry, the trip was soon behind them, and although something of an adventure, the children had no idea when they would see Mums and Dads again. Days passed. William and Kitty's group was soon homesick and disoriented. After the train journey they were based in a school hall somewhere up north, where each was given an identification number and eventually passed on to be billeted with a local family. Two months passed quickly. They were away from it all, but occasionally saw vapour trails in the sky as friendly and enemy aircraft fought one another high above distant cities. And on a still night the 'crumping' sound of distant bombing made them huddle together in bed.

Back home it was an entirely different story. Time and again William and Kitty's parents joined others in the underground rail stations when air attack sirens ordered immediate evacuation of buildings and streets. There were often numerous visits during the course of a day, and sometimes it became the safest place to spend the whole night.

Life went on as best it could amongst death and misery. Faces turned towards the shelter ceilings as bombs landed closer and closer. Waiting, listening, praying. Faces reflecting the fear this daily threat had over the city's people. These were lonely hours when parents thought of their youngsters. Hoping they were safe, far away, and never likely to experience this type of danger. Finally emerging to be confronted by the dreadful mayhem around them, and the risk of more to come from unexploded bombs just waiting to be accidentally triggered. Many found themselves unable to cope, and yet one by one they pulled themselves together, rallied, and with renewed spirit carried on with a burning determination that Britain would eventually win.

One night enemy planes sneaked in under a low canopy of rain cloud. At the very last minute the bombers were picked up by radar, but this time they had too much of a head start for an air raid warning to be effective. The deafening sounds became apparent as people rushed from their homes, with many never reaching allocated shelters in time. It was a night of terror, noise and catastrophic destruction. Hundreds died.

William and Kitty were fortunate to have stayed together, and they adapted well to their new countryside surroundings. Like other evacuees, they were not immediately informed when their parents died during a bombing raid. No word came through at the time. It was rather hectic with the war of course. Divorced from the visual effect of burning buildings, houses chopped in half with all their rooms exposed, and streets blocked by rubble that once represented safe homes, the children playfully shot one another with makeshift weapons and continued to be just kids. In this corner of England, for them at least, fun, guns and chasing games were normal fare. Disrupted services meant the news was not conveyed to their guardians until many weeks later.

Thinking back, Bill vaguely remembered a day when they all cried. All the members of the foster family were upset. There seemed no reason at the time, but he guessed later that was when he and Kitty officially became orphans. The years passed and both kids had a number of birthdays with what they had come to regard as being 'their family'. Really, William had little recollection of those days. What he remembered was, in most cases, what Kitty had been able to recall at some later stage. She had told him they were both well looked after by their new parents, and cared for as if they were their own. Kitty's birthday was 17 November, his a week earlier. It had taken time before she had accepted that, although older, his birthday always came first.

The meeting was in a stone church. He could remember that. But only just. It marked the start of an adventure beyond anyone's comprehension. There were twenty or thirty families and many children involved. They all had to listen in silence. You could have heard a pin drop as the officials talked at length. None of the kids could follow the detail, but it was explained to them later that there was to be a better life ahead for everyone. A long journey to a gracious green and pleasant land. A place that consisted of sheep and farmers. A 'scenic wonder', whatever that was, and a visitor's delight. It all sounded marvellous to the older children.

The foster family was sad to be losing them after such a long stretch. About one hundred kids all told were to be permanently relocated in New Zealand. While William and Kitty and many other kids had wanted to stay put, regrettably the children had no say in the matter. Ironically, those remaining behind, for whatever reason, came to regard the selected ones with a little envy. The day of departure drew near. Bill had become used to his new nickname, and at six, almost seven years of age, and with Kitty two years older, their lives changed once again.

Local newspapers throughout October 1950 heralded the ship's impending arrival. Stories headed 'displaced persons' brought huge crowds to the wharves on the day to watch the immigrant ship *Hellenic Prince* trying to berth. It was one of the largest boats to arrive for months and the tugs had difficulty controlling it in the Wellington wind. During the trip out the children had learned a lot about New Zealand, and with friendships fostered on board, thoughts of those left behind had diminished. Lining the railings, they strained now for their first glimpse of this longed-for country. It was a chilly day, but clear, and the distant perimeter of Wellington was dotted with inner city buildings and houses. Some high up had commanding views out over the harbour and beyond Somes Island, while others marked the shore line. There were a hundred or so children without parents on board. When it came time to disembark, the group's chaperones quickly ushered them from gang-plank to wharf and into a designated building for processing. Some in the same family were split up, but William and Kitty's luck held out. They remained together, holding hands tightly amid the confusion as records were slowly sorted. The system seemed to be all to hell, and as hours passed officials looked down on faces etched with tiredness and prayed for continued calm. There were tearful kids, especially the younger ones. It was all beyond Bill's comprehension, but for Kitty things were relatively normal. She had become conditioned to being passed from person to person and place to place. These days she was very accepting of constant uncertainty and of receiving instructions from different adults. And while sometimes she spoke out, in the main Kitty simply did as she was told.

Things improved later in the day when some semblance of order appeared to take place up front. The queue began to move more quickly, and then it was off to camp for two weeks until the day of allocation. Most of them suffered badly from the change of climate and diet during this period. It was a wretched fortnight. Finally the day they had waited so long for dawned, and dozens of children once again stood patiently in line until individual names were called through the speaker system.

'William and Kitty Wilson,' came the announcement.

Everyone had been given his or her New Zealand foster parent's surname. There was no other 'William and Kitty' as such, and being at the head of the line they stepped forward with confidence. The Wilsons waved enthusiastically at what seemed to them to be two lost souls. A couple of ginger-headed waifs who were clearly of small build for their ages.

'Hullo, Kitty and William.'

'It's Bill,' he mumbled to Mr and Mrs Wilson, trying to say it with a smile at the same time. His mates had started calling him Bill just prior to the trip. He liked it and it had stuck.

'Good morning Mr and Mrs Wilson,' replied Kitty with a solemn look on her face. Everything seemed very formal and awkward during these initial moments.

Mr Wilson and Bill carried their gear to the bus stop. Kitty and their new Mum walked on ahead hand in hand. The Wilsons explained that they had left their car at the nearest town to their home, and that while petrol rationing had been lifted, the use of public transport for longer trips such as this one had become second nature to them.

'Things are changing back to the way they were before the war, but oh so slowly,' Mrs Wilson told them. 'We've got no children of our own, and live in a place called the Wairarapa valley.' It was a disjointed conversation but a way of giving the kids an overall picture of what lay ahead. Bill had some trouble getting his tongue around the name Wairarapa. Too many R's in it or something.

The Wilsons were pleased when the words 'Mum' and 'Dad' occasionally slipped into the conversation as naturally as anything, and with interest expressed in how the trip out had gone the conversation progressed more easily. A lot of time was spent answering questions, so much so that the city's suburbs and new countryside almost passed unnoticed. It was a slow bus trip that took them up over the Rimutakas, a central ridge of hills that divides the lower North Island in half. Kitty was sick because of the long winding route. They stopped twice for her but the driver seemed not to mind the delay. Each time it was a chance to let his bus cool down a bit. The engine smelled hot, and the radiator had been spitting too. Long stains of brown water were evident on the bodywork when they stopped for a breather, and a hot puddle of steaming water on the ground each time they moved on left proof of that. At the top, Bill and Kitty had their first opportunity for a peep at the flat farmland they were heading for.

The green Wairarapa lay before them in all its glory. It was a greenness quite unlike that of England. Perhaps not so much the colour as it was the vast openness. Although only vaguely remembering, and barely able to compare, Kitty recalled pictures of undulating land with small fields linking to form a patchwork quilt-like design of colours and shapes. The thick hawthorn hedges had helped create that effect. Different crops, the type of stock on individual farmlets, the shadows and sunlight. All these contributed to the English scene. Over here the countryside was not divided into such uniformity. This valley seemed to spread forever, with little in the way of division. There was a different style of fencing too.

'It's been like this for a while now. Rather beautiful and lush isn't it? It's a valley that's yet to feel the full effect of New Zealand's heat. We'll see some changes soon when it gets really hot,' Mr Wilson added. 'And this is the start of the Tararua range I was telling you about earlier.' He referred back to a conversation when they were leaving Upper Hutt, when they could just make out distant tree damage from an old fire on the Marchant ridge. He had been describing the forest park, and how it stretched to the north covering almost 400,000 acres. 'We're very lucky today because most of the time it's shrouded in mist. In fact, they say the tops are fog-bound two out of every three days.'

Both kids stared out at the view, unsure as to whether the feelings they had were of being homesick or just an eagerness for what adventures lay ahead. Mr Wilson had already told of the trees near their house where Bill could build a hut, and he had responded with enthusiasm, chatting away and asking all manner of questions. Kitty on the other hand remained quiet. Content to just listen, it seemed. She was not feeling very well anyway, so that had to be taken into consideration. War was unfair, especially on kids like her. While craving security, attention and parental love herself, the responsibility placed on her for looking after her younger brother had shown from time to time, and the weeks on board had seemed endless. The trip out to New Zealand had not been a comfortable one. It had been a very thankful Kitty who walked off the ship, pleased to finally relinquish her semi-child minding role, and ready to return to being a kid herself.

Along the way people had assumed the little girl had been coping, but inside she had been lost. The fact they had lived with other families in England, and then at a time when things had seemed to be getting better had to come out here, well it had all been a bit too much for her. Lately she had rarely expressed an opinion, and appeared comfortable just to be drawn along with the crowd. Mrs Wilson put a motherly arm around her, and said in a quiet aside to her husband, 'Perhaps she'll come to life after we've put this last part of the trip behind us.'

As expected, the hilltop delay was beneficial, and Kitty felt better for the fresh air. After twenty minutes or so some colour returned to her cheeks. It dawned on her as they reboarded the bus that it was her ninth birthday and that Bill had forgotten. So too had she until just then. So much happening today.

Bill had no trouble calling him 'Dad'. Mr Wilson was a farm labourer and did a lot of tractor work, and Bill told him he hoped to learn to drive farm machinery one day too. A father and son-like bond seemed well on its way to being established. Both kids had experienced constant change during the past few years, and there had been some expected effects. Bed-wetting and nightmares aboard the ship had not been uncommon. Those problems soon stopped however. Mum and Dad Wilson seemed a warm and cuddly couple, and in the short time they had all been together both kids could feel normality returning to their lives.

'You've not got too far to walk to your new school, you kids,' said Mum. 'It's small, and your teacher is someone we know well.'

'Only three miles each way,' Dad added with a grin.

Bill and Kitty were used to making friends, and the thought of new surroundings was not at all daunting.

'Nearly there,' Dad said when they climbed down from the bus. 'Just a short trip from here.'

The Wilson's car was parked in the main street of Greytown, a rural township with quaint colonial homes dotted about amongst the newer ones. The car was a 1938 Morris 8. A blue and black one with only two doors. Although they had been in the country a couple of weeks already, this was their first opportunity to have a decent look at the shops. They had their first New Zealand ice-creams right there and then at the local general store. Chocolate ones in pink cones. Unfortunately, within a mile it was all Kitty needed to help her throw up yet again.

It did not take very long from the outskirts of town to home. Another windy road. A dusty one this time, but they took it very slowly. Even so, Kitty was pleased to get out of the car at the end of it all, for the day had been hard on her stomach and her throat was raw. Neither of them had envisaged living in a house where neighbours could not actually be heard or seen. It was going to be strange for a while. But right from the start Bill loved it. He stood on the grassed-over driveway drinking in the scene. This was not a house, it was his new home, and he loved the feel of the place. Loved the way it sat there all old and quaint, surrounded by lush green hills rising behind it. And those trees. So big.

'Our own bedrooms and chests of drawers,' Kitty shouted from inside. She was first in the house. No need to lock doors around here.

'Can I have this one, Mum?' she asked before Bill even had a chance to view either of them. So much for feeling ill and not helping bring in the cases and things. 'Girls,' he thought.

Mum agreed without hesitation. It did not matter either way, they were both nice rooms. Kitty's was next to Mum and Dad's, Bill's at the other end off the lounge.

Their belongings easily fitted in the top drawers alone. Bill stuffed his things in, along with a letter from their old Mum. Something written in haste prior to being sent away by train. And a parcel from his old Dad to be opened one day in the future. Just a couple of treasures from the past. They had arrived with one pair of shoes each and a change of clothes. Kitty had a coat.

'It won't be long before we need to get you both fitted out properly,' Mum said with a bit of a look on her face. 'We thought you would have come over with a more appropriate range of clothing for our weather.'

Both kids looked forward to that shopping expedition which was eventually planned for the following week.

The adjustment was not too hard, and the different style of schooling here never looked like posing a problem. Both thrived, and in next to no time felt like born and bred New Zealanders. And then in a wink the first couple of years slipped by.

In 1952 they were still being ribbed by schoolmates about their accents, but that was all right. Even years later, they would still be referred to as the 'new kids' or 'little Poms'. Little, because next to any other kids in their classes they looked frail in comparison. It was probably that lack of good wholesome food during the infant years when England's wartime rationing was still in place. Next to Bertha in particular Kitty was like a human doll, but then again Bertha was big by any standards. Her parents were dairy farmers, and she was always being teased in class about her weight. Whether it was at school or elsewhere in the district, Bill did not mind being called the pommie kid. But Kitty sometimes took exception to the slang term if feeling out of sorts. Living in England seemed a long time back now. They were both very happy, well loved, and felt healthy and strong. Mr Wilson had taught Bill how to wrestle. A bit of a skinny wrestler, but that hardly mattered.

CHAPTER 3

It had become a daily ritual checking the bathroom mirror. Peering at the face looking back at him and searching for pimples. Studying the freckles and convincing himself they were fading.

'When did yours go?' he called to Kitty in the other room. She would know what he was talking about. Actually he could not remember her ever having freckles, so was not really listening for an answer.

'Don't know,' came the reply without the least bit of concern in her voice. 'Wish I had some though'. He could tell the sarcastic tone, and visualised a mocking look on her face.

Mrs Wilson struggled up the steps. It was her washing day.

'This is heavy, come lend a hand with the sorting dears. I could hear you two red-heads from the yard you know. Don't for the life of me know why you go on so, Bill. They may be gone next week, they may be there forever. There are more important things in life to consider than looks.'

He scowled at the mild scolding, but had nothing to say.

'We're off to the shops soon. You two can come with me. I'm meeting the ladies at 10.30 a.m. so a quick wash and best behaviour today.'

'As if she needed to ask,' he thought.

'What a waste of a day,' Bill mumbled, and Kitty agreed. Anyway they felt resigned to the shopping, and consoled themselves with the hope of an ice-cream.

Their road was still a gravel one, with little chance of it ever being upgraded. Neither kid minded the drive these days, as it took little time once underway. But the boredom associated with this type of visit usually showed on the two glum faces, and the trip today was no exception.

'It's not so much the shopping, Mum, but more the silly talk those ladies have. Lots of dumb questions needing polite answers. A whole morning can be gabbed away if you aren't careful.'

Mrs Wilson smiled at him, remembering the times when both kids enjoyed attention from her friends. But she realised too that a boy soon seeks recognition for qualities other than spelling test results, and all those things adults seemed to place great store in. She knew their comments about cute freckles and how tall he had grown was the stuff for babies, and that they were both well past that stage.

'Are you going to be long today, Mum?' Kitty pleaded. 'We have to meet the other kids later,' she went on, emphasising the 'have to'. Mrs Wilson smiled again. She had no idea what delays might be experienced. There was always someone uptown, and it was important to keep in touch with local news. From Bill's point of view, they never discussed interesting things. None of them. He had little to share with older women, so usually just tried to be as inconspicuous as possible.

Three or four 'oldies' had formed a group outside the dress shop next to Smetherton's dairy. They were exchanging pleasantries with those coming and going, and admiring new season materials on display. Mrs Wilson joined them, and the group nattered amongst themselves, practically ignoring the two kids this time. Patience was not one of Bill's greatest attributes at his age, and he soon resorted to kicking out the front of his shoe against the curb in the hope it would hasten things along.

'These kids are waiting for something from Dulcies,' she eventually explained, while looking in the direction of the sweet shop. They moved on to the corner dairy, but only after the usual goodbyes during which one or two new topics of conversation were started.

Usually they could conjure up some excuse for not helping with weekly shopping, and as a consequence spent much of their time with others of a similar age. The kids made the most of their rural playground, loving the freedom, the peace and the fresh air. While a bit slow off the mark today, they both knew they would escape shortly after lunch and have the rest of the day to do as they liked.

• • • • • • •

'Isn't this a great place?'

Kitty always spoke with such enthusiasm. You could hear it in her voice, and sometimes Bill just sat back and listened to her talk like a grown-up. They could smell summer in the warmth of the ground. Even at this young age it filled their heads with memories of previous Januarys they had already enjoyed here.

'This is exactly what it was like last year — that smell of warm dusty grass, these perfectly blue skies.'

The kids gathered long grass about them, each in their own makeshift nest. Just lying there watching as two hawks tracked back and forth above them, and straining to hear the birds' distant cries. It was the only disturbance in the stillness of the day. Kitty shielded her eyes from the sunlight, and let the other three know when they eventually flew off over the ridge.

With that distraction now behind them, she made an announcement.

'I'm going to sleep right here where we are.'

The others agreed it would be nice but everyone realised it was something that would be unacceptable to their parents. And besides, not long after dusk the grass would be wet with dew from the cold night air.

'Have you brought them with you, Ben?' Bill called, ignoring any further comments from his sister. Ben was lying out of view from them, just below the others.

'I'd be surprised if you didn't,' he continued. 'You're always flogging the stuff. It's a wonder you've never been caught. Then again your Dad's damn near blind isn't he?'

While Ben and Abel were older by about a year, and little Kitty older again, they tended to accept Bill, the youngest and skinniest of them all, as being the unofficial leader of their gang. As usual, Ben had a supply of tobacco and papers with him and began making up a fag. His father was unaware of small amounts missing from his leather pouch. They all lit up. Even Kitty had a puff. An apple, later on, would help disguise any smell on their breath. Bill was not to know then that this was the start of a smoking habit that would last the rest of his life.

Sounds of voices brought all four of them back to their senses.

'Can't see anyone,' said Ben, rising cautiously from his position further down the slope.

'Keep down for God's sake.' Bill had not meant to hiss the words so sternly through clenched teeth. Ben dropped out of sight but was visibly upset. He had a really bad complexion, and his pimply skin quivered as he whispered his response back to Bill.

'I sometimes think you only invite me along for the smokes.'

'They'll see you from that angle,' Bill hastened to explain, softening his tone. He hoped Ben could see he was concerned for him as well.

'If they get up here, they'll be looking for a fight, Ben. Probably smack Kitty up too.'

They slipped down to where he lay and studied the terrain below. While this was not their orchard, and they were trespassing themselves, they had long regarded it as being their fruit for the taking.

A line of older boys emerged from the creek bed. There were nine of them, and they were having some difficulty negotiating the tangle of blackberries. In any event, they were too preoccupied to notice Bill's group lurking on the slope above. Some were familiar faces. The others were newcomers.

'Look, they're armed with sacks and a box.'

It was clear they were intent on filching a fair amount of fruit. The thought of 'outsiders' raiding the last of the apples was too much, and Bill's group quickly withdrew a few yards and planned their attack.

'We're outnumbered,' Kitty contributed, hoping they could simply slip away unnoticed.

Not only were they younger, but also Ben's group were disadvantaged by Kitty's presence. It went without saying. After all she was only a girl. But Kitty was right, no matter what the circumstances, it was going to be difficult.

'Listen,' Bill hissed firmly, taking control. Once again he surprised himself at the sternness in his voice. 'At least we have the element of surprise in our favour. And there's also the advantage of our position and an easy escape route.'

'And at least they don't have any dogs with them,' continued Kitty with a slightly more confident tone.

They all hated dogs. Especially excited ones. The dog Bill and Kitty sometimes looked after was gentle and quiet and would be lying in the sun at home. Other people's animals always seemed to run wild.

'Piece of piss,' Abel announced, by way of confirmation that indeed they did have the upper hand.

It was an expression he loved to use when there were no grown-ups around. Full of confidence as always.

'Piece of piss,' they all chorused.

'This should be fun.'

They pulled back even further. And once well out of sight they set to, amassing a pile of ammo. Windfall apples lay in the hundreds. It was merely a matter of collecting them into handy piles.

The first the intruders knew they were not alone was when a hail of missiles began to hit the dirt around them. They certainly had the range, but none was particularly accurate. There were few direct hits. They pelted the group with all their strength, effectively stopping the enemy in their tracks. The older boys backed off out of range with cries of indignation. They could do little more than hurl insults in return.

'We can see ya Bill Wilson,' came a voice from below. 'Just wait 'til we get up there, ya sod.'

There was much shouting from below, and Bill's group matched it with taunting laughter. The air rang with battle cries as their next salvo was launched. Then there was a pause while everyone regrouped and repositioned themselves. As expected the older ones advanced from below, and this time their determination showed.

Bill felt it necessary to introduce different tactics and called his team into a huddle. He quickly explained how months earlier, while sitting around the fire at home, Dad had told him and Kitty stories of the Boer war. Of how the British soldiers had kept hordes of Zulu warriors at bay. Thousands of them. Bill remembered his explanation of how the British would line up in three ranks. The front row would fire, then kneel and reload while the second rank fired then knelt. By the time the third lot had fired, and followed the procedure, the first were ready to stand again, and so it went on. A steady hail of shot.

'We have to do this in an orderly fashion,' said Bill, mimicking his Dad.

Some ground was given away as they gathered even more apples. A large pile was required. Kitty kept a watch on the advancing group. Then with only yards between them, but on higher ground, they finally let fly as a group, then fell into a pattern of shot after shot. Bill repositioned them as soon as the advancing foe began to falter.

'Ben, you stand there because you're the stronger thrower.' He was trying to retrieve the situation, following his earlier harshness towards his friend.

'Your bowling ability makes you the better shot,' he continued in encouragement.

It was a fact. Their local cricket team never won against other teams, but regardless they had some good players. Ben was the school's best, and everyone lived in hope of a team win one day.

'Front row fire,' Bill yelled at Kitty and Abel. 'Second row fire,' and Ben let loose. Bill was third, and when throwing his apple, more by accident than anything else, scored a direct hit as the group tried ineffectively to close on them. At this range their aim was true, and the apples rained down relentlessly. The enemy returned some fire but was soon forced back to the creek again and out of range. It had all been rather spectacular and very effective.

Four pairs of eyes watched as the older boys searched the creek bed and retrieved apples. Appropriately armed, they spread themselves out along the base of the slope and headed upwards. Advancing slowly, throwing insults as the gap closed, it was clear they were saving their run for the last moment. Bill's lot simply did not have the numbers to hold off such a widespread attack.

The older boys all ducked as those at the top each let fly a couple of shots. Then, in an instant, and as if prearranged, there was an opportunity to escape back over the brow of the hill and Bill's group took it. A silence became apparent. An eerie silence that dragged on for ages.

'They're probably still creeping up and not really sure where we'll pop out from.'

They laughed loudly as they ran. It was one of those days they would all think back on with a chuckle in years to come. They had won the battle. Life was good.

It was a roundabout way of leaving the orchard. The foursome rejoined the road a good half-hour from home. No doubt there would be numerous distractions. These country roads were littered with bits and pieces worthy of inspection.

'Here's someone's milk-churn lid,' said Kitty, kicking it off into the paspalum, a common weed that lined these rural routes.

The boys saw from the start it was a hubcap, and a heated discussion took place as to its origin. It was impossible for them to walk any distance in silence. There was always some topic they could argue to death.

'The weather's turning.'

In the short space of time since they had lain in the sun a cold wind had whipped up. As if a signal of worse to come, they all began to run. Abel and Ben peeled off at their respective gates.

'See yah tomorrow.'

'Yeah, you too.'

Kitty and Bill walked briskly from then on. It was not too far, although there was a shortcut worth considering. The darkening sky hurried their pace again, and they chose the shorter route as the first patter of rain disturbed the dusty gravel. Fresh rain on a dry road has a smell of its own. A smell Bill loved. One of his favourite aromas.

They were now on a well-worn track through a maze of lupin bushes. There were various options, but to the uninitiated these tracks would have had you running in circles. You needed to know the system.

'Slow down, Bill,' Kitty pleaded.

There was a squealing urgency in her voice when she repeated it a moment later. It made him slow the pace and she quickly caught up.

'It's all right for you being in front, but these wet branches hurt when they flick back.'

'I'm protecting you by getting rid of the wet, otherwise you'd be soaked by now.'

'I'm soaked already, you dummy.'

Bill stopped, and held up his finger to hush her noise. They moved on silently, giving Holloway's cottage a wide berth. His dogs were vicious, but today they appeared not to have detected them and they were soon past the house. Perhaps the wind was working in their favour. They eventually heard the hounds protesting vigorously behind them, finally catching the intruders' scent and snatching at their chains as they assumed their guard dog roles. Then the heavens opened, and chucked all that could be mustered in a short but drenching downpour.

The Wilsons had told them right back at the start that this was nature's way of cleansing the countryside. It turned dust-covered scrub from grey back to green. Bill was not so much worried about getting wet as he was about getting his blade rusty. That knife was one of his most treasured possessions. And really his only remaining link to his real parents, other than Kitty. Santa had given it to him the previous Christmas. He learned later it had been in the parcel that had accompanied them, but had been kept aside until he was old enough.

Mum was still a bit concerned he would not appreciate the responsibility that went with owning such a thing. It had a silver skull and crossbones mounted in the bone handle, and that alone made it look really impressive. That and the gold studs. It was also a bit bigger than any of the knives his friends had, and a 'two-blader'. And both were razor sharp. All other gifts that Christmas had come second by comparison. Finding it safely in his pocket, he ran his thumb over the 'skull'. It was a habit he had adopted from the start. A way of reassuring himself it was still with him. As a result, the 'skull' had already become smooth and shiny. That Christmas, his stocking had been full of presents. Even got an orange. She had done it the previous year too. Stocking-fillers, his Mum would call them. Some types of fruit were not always so plentiful, and something like that was a bit of a treat. They always had plums and peaches from the trees out the back, but somehow oranges were always in short supply. The first thing Bill had done was carve the peel off. Made a real state of his bedding. Juice everywhere, and cut himself too. He did not care though. That knife was going to go everywhere with him from that day on.

Both were breathless when they got to the back porch. Bill cleaned both blades on his shirt, and made a mental note to oil them later. They stood there, soaked from hair to shoes.

'Probably best to let our gear dry out here,' Bill said, putting his shoes up on the shelf where the dog could not get at them. Dad had already had one accident with boots. A right chewed-up mess they had been.

'Remember we've been told not to play in that orchard.' They could hear their Mum inside, but before agreeing on the same story the door was flung open.

'About time too,' she said, looking at clothing that would have to be dried on the rack above the stove. 'You should be ashamed of yourself, Bill. You should have got Kitty home well before this rain.'

While Kitty was older, Bill was always regarded as being in charge. That was what being the boy was all about, he had been told once. Mrs Wilson held him responsible for Kitty whenever they were playing away from home. They squeezed past her without a word, pleased to get into the warm.

'Straight to your rooms now and change. And nothing wet left on the floor,' she called after them. 'Just look at you.'

Bill heard the words through the wall of his room. He could tell from her voice she was angry, and also from the way she fussed about gathering up grass-stained and sodden clothing from both rooms. He returned, and sat quietly in front of the fire in his dressing gown. When she eventually calmed down he told her of the day's adventure. It was best to tell the truth.

He always did anyway, and while she said nothing about trespassing, her expression showed it was clearly something that did not meet with her approval.

Later he slipped off to use the water Kitty had finished with. No waste in this house.

They had been so dirty it had been off to the washhouse to bathe. An awkward climb up high to get into the concrete tub next to the old wood-burning copper, but worth the effort.

'Won't be long and I won't fit into this. It's either getting narrower, or I'm getting bigger,' he joked at her through the wall. It was still nice and deep and he sank into its depths, manoeuvring himself past the taps for a good long soak. Even with shoulder blades rubbing against the rough unforgiving surface it was lovely, and Bill could have stayed there all night.

'I'm going to climb up to the trig station tomorrow and take a look around,' he called out.

There was no response so he assumed no one had heard him. It would be good to go up to the highest point around here for perhaps a last look at the view. The way their Dad had been talking lately, it was likely they would be moving on soon.

CHAPTER 4

The Wilsons had lived there for a long time. Originally built as a shearer's cottage, it had become cheap, temporary accommodation for a number of families over the years.

Between occupants it had lain empty, with locals referring to it for many years as 'the haunted house'. Ancient macrocarpas, with trunks so large that two men would have had difficulty reaching around with outstretched arms, cast ominous shadows over the property, blocking out much of the daylight. It certainly gave the impression of being an eerie dwelling on a bad day. What a difference, people had remarked in the past, if someone could remove a few of the trees to let in more light. But no one was ever likely to attempt such a task.

'Temporary' had lasted six years for the Wilsons prior to the kids' arrival. Theirs was the only visible hint of civilisation this end of the valley. The house had been built on a sunny site many years previously, but its shelter belt had grown too high. Little in the way of warmth got through to the grounds these days. Just a bit each morning. Some would have regarded it as being in a state of disrepair, but to Bill and Kitty it was home, and the Wilson family had done a lot to make it feel like a good place to live. It was basically a fenced-off, unused corner of a larger run-down farm.

Long before Bill and Kitty arrived on the scene, the Wilsons had moved from place to place at will, never lasting more than a month or so in any one spot. Eventually they found this home, as well as employment in the area. While they had yearned for a family of their own over the years, luck had not been on their side. The chance to foster a couple of needy kids was taken without hesitation. They saw it as reward for showing some stability in their lives at last.

'Perhaps we've finally got that element of gypsy out of our blood,' Mrs Wilson had said at the time. But here they were, once more considering another move. Bill was not privy to detail, but he wondered if the farmer his Dad worked for simply could not afford the cost of an extra man. Perhaps it would be good to move to a different house. He loved the home they had, but temperature-wise it had always been rather cold.

Being almost dwarfed by shrubbery probably did not help the situation. A wild rose had completely covered the lean-to portion of the house, and looked ready to take over the nearby shed as well. That shed was full of wetas they had been told, and Bill and Kitty had always steered well clear of it. In any case it was dark and scary, and with their youthful imaginations they envisaged it as being a convenient hidey-hole for some escaped convict covered in blood and wrapped in chains. When they had first confessed their fear of the shed a year or so back, Mrs Wilson just put it down to being one of those things associated with adjusting to new surroundings. Because it was never dismissed as out and out silliness, the apprehension carried on so that, even today, both kids and their friends gave it a wide berth. Ben had told them people in general had always considered the property haunted, but that they were possibly just referring to that shed in particular.

Bill remembered the first time they had seen a weta. It had been sitting quietly on Kitty's jersey after they emerged from the bush. It looked like a very large grasshopper. But when he tried to remove it, those menacing barbed legs were raised defensively, and its nippers looked really dangerous. He had thought better of it. Kitty had screamed all the way back to the house where Mum calmly flicked it off, quick as anything, and then squashed it with her foot. While the thought of a room full of them had kept both kids away from the shed, the rotting structure had almost fallen down anyway, and that too was as much a deterrent.

Encroaching bush gave the house a slight dampness you could smell inside. They somehow looked past the faint aroma, but it was noticeable to any others who visited. Also on the down side, they were just over an hour's walk from the cluster of shops they called town, so most of the time the car was required. But on a positive note, the house was well back, providing peaceful seclusion. Its driveway also distanced them from any dust churned up by farm vehicles, and what little other traffic was using the road.

Saturday mornings were busy at the best of times, and it was unusual to get away from the many chores around the place. This morning was different however.

'My goodness, look at that long face. Off you go. Don't want glum kids around here today. When there's work to be done later, I'll call you both. I'll want to see some smiles then, too.'

Kitty was happy to just sit in the sun by the clothesline. She knew the patch of warmth would not remain for long, but Bill took the opportunity while he had it, heading for his favourite vantage point. It took only five minutes, and from there he looked back and could just see his mum emptying the teapot into the hydrangeas at the back porch. Fingers of sunlight were reaching the house at last, having crept across the yard towards her. He wondered if spider webs were still glistening in the hedge down there. From the trees came a sound, and Bill knew his mum would be listening to the same musical squawking that he could hear from up here at the trig. Magpies heralding a new day.

She moved from the steps, shaking crumbs from her tablecloth as she went. A jovial woman, their mum. Taking all the family's problems in her stride. Rarely complaining. There were regular reasons for complaint, however, for while they were pretty undemanding kids, times were hard, and there was never any extra money in the house. Each Thursday was payday. Single income of course, and not that great an amount. The mail kept bringing letters about overdue bills, and often it seemed to Bill they were hard-pressed covering basic living costs. Most of the time all this stuff went well above their heads, but just occasionally the kids were aware of difficulties.

'We need to start afresh somewhere else,' Dad had explained. 'How do you feel about a new school? Bigger one and better. Lots more friends.'

Bill was still resentful. A chain rattling down below distracted him. It was barely audible. The dog had sensed Mrs Wilson's presence and emerged from his den under the shed. Just a hole under the floor. Wetas were no problem for him. Muzzle greyed by the brush of time, eyes sad but always with a trusting look, the animal stretched in the warmth of the morning, then continued wagging his tail with the pleasure of seeing her. It was an action that moved his whole hindquarters. He was not theirs. They were just minding him for the week, but he treated them as if they were his family, and it was obvious he relished any attention given to him from kids and adults alike.

In the driveway the Wilson's Morris 8 and trailer were half-packed. Although just a youngster, Bill had been quite vocal the night before. He had made his displeasure at the proposed move very clear. Kitty had the same mates, but did not seem as concerned as he at severing those ties. She was hoping for friends more her own age than the ones around here. The likelihood of better work for their Dad was greater elsewhere. And when all was said and done, that had to be the deciding factor.

'It'll be the last we ever see of rabbit snaring, eeling and diving in a decent swimming hole,' Bill had argued.

In the end he had to resign himself to the fact that he might well have raided his last orchard too. Yes, last night's discussion had been a bit strained.

Leaning against the trig station, constructed years ago for survey purposes on this highest point, he had a last look out across the valley and beyond. Off to his left, sheep were forming lines across the slopes. They slowly followed each other, and headed towards remaining patches of shade. It was shaping up to be a hot day. Some paddocks were emerald green and lush, in part the result of regular rainfall lately — not something that was ever constant in the Wairarapa. Others patches of ground had been well-chewed, and would have difficulty recovering from the condition they had been left in. Bill could tell which farmers had given proper thought to stock rotation. He took a last look at the initials he had carved in the wood the first day he arrived here. His thumb caressed the shape of the skull in the handle. It was a comfort knowing his knife was nestled safely in his pocket. He heard his name being called way off in the distance and headed down the slope.

Arriving back at the house, he found Kitty carting burnable rubbish to the outside incinerator beyond the sheds.

'Dad's got the bonnet up. There's something wrong with the general-later,' she declared.

'Girls,' he mumbled to himself. 'Haven't got a clue.'

'It's a generator Kitty, and it's to do with the electrics.'

Mr Wilson had nothing to say for a long time. In fact, he struggled under the bonnet for over an hour before giving up. It seemed the engine problems were not going to be rectified easily.

As the day neared its end, wisps of smoke from the wood-burning stove signalled suppertime and they settled back into their routine.

'In a way, it's good to be spending a night in rooms with familiar smells,' Mum said.

Kitty agreed for both of them, giving Bill a wink and a playful punch for good measure. There was no unpacking of the trailer for two days. Just mattresses on the floors. Then everything came back inside, and before they knew it a few more months had passed.

There was still no casual work on the farm so Mr Wilson moved from general farm work to duties at a local saw mill. The farmer they had rented from for so long was not that worried about the situation, so they simply stayed put.

Mr Wilson hunted out a magnifying glass from his belongings. It had come to light when packing for the planned move.

'Here you are, Bill. That's for doing so well with the firewood.'

They now had a pile that would do them for many months, and in an idle moment Bill used his new acquisition to burn his initials on the veranda boards. WW. While he was known only as Bill, the initials for William Wilson looked more impressive. It was just good luck that Mum was in the front room and able to smell the wisps of smoke. She came running, and found him focusing the rays of the sun on the wooden planks.

'What on earth... stop that at once you silly, silly, stupid boy!'

It was probably the first time she had really growled. Unaware that tinder-dry grass under the steps could so easily have set the whole place on fire, he came very close to having his new treasure confiscated.

It was 1953. An important year with lots of memories to look back on later. The country had a new Queen and that had brought back thoughts of England, especially when they saw photographs in the newspaper. Edmund Hillary had climbed Mount Everest in July. There was a photo of him in the paper too. A New Zealander standing on top of the world and holding a flag. They had had a light dusting of snow that year. On his tenth birthday Bill had made a flag and gone up to pose by the trig. It was well and truly dry by then of course, but Dad went too and took a 'snap' with his box Brownie camera. Bill pinned the photo on his bedroom wall, and it became another of his prized possessions.

From time to time they would go to the pictures as a family. They always dressed up and regarded it as being a real treat. There was a theatre in the next town so it was some drive to get there and back. Bill loved the 'westerns'.

'Wasn't it a great shoot-out, Dad? The best part was when the baddy thought he had got the good guy and came out of hiding too early.'

'Yes son,' Mr Wilson said, 'in situations like that one, someone invariably makes a mistake. It's a bit like hunting. You need great patience. Always remember that Bill... patience.'

The weather remained settled for weeks, and the warmth reminded them again of those 'apple raiding' summer days ages ago.

'The morning shadows seem to know not to linger too long,' said their father as he sat nursing his second cup of tea for the day. 'I'd say it's going to be a good one,' he continued thoughtfully. Their lawn, dew-covered at 6.00 a.m., had progressed through that steaming period when brief patches of sun had eventually hit it, and the grass was now fairly dry. There was not a cloud to be seen. It was one of those rare, high blue skies. Absolutely flawless.

'It's the type of day that makes you wish something had been planned for it,' Mum ventured.

'There's no Saturday work for Dad today,' she said with no thought as to how that might affect their finances, 'so how about a picnic?'

The way the conversation was going, both Kitty and Bill wondered whether it had all been planned in advance. There was much discussion, and they finally agreed on what would be taken and where they would go. With packed lunch and fishing gear they ambled down the road a few hundred yards, left the paddocks behind them, and entered the cool of the bush. In places natural dampness steamed in the warmth of the morning, and all around a thousand cicadas deafened them with their noise. The track was slippery, but then again it was always muddy through there.

'Watch it up ahead, you'll have to go around those boggy bits.'

There were places in the path that could suck your boots off. And would do so, given the chance. It had happened more than once before, so both kids knew which of the many routes to take and they led the way. It was a well-trodden track to the water hole. Their water hole. And it was while they lunched there in the grass beside the creek that they learned of Dad's news.

'Your Aunt Tilly and her husband are to pay us a visit from Australia. They're selling up and coming out here to live permanently,' he said. 'Haven't seen my sister for years and years,' he continued fondly.

Bill was pleased for him. He could see the delight in his Dad's face, and thought of what it might have been like if Kitty and he had been separated. One of them here and one over there.

Aunt Tilly was Dad's older sister. Having married Jim Dwyer, they had gone off to the Australian outback years ago and successfully farmed a large property. To all accounts, theirs had been a good and happy life, but it was unfortunate they had not had a family of their own to share it with. The couple was now looking for a new challenge.

'But with Tilly feeling somewhat frail, they're considering their options carefully,' their father explained. 'They're looking for a change of climate, and plan to spend a few weeks over here in a month's time. Hope to get a feel for the area during their visit, so we may be seeing a lot of them in the years to come. Especially if they settle down around here.'

Bill vaguely remembered some adverse comments his Dad had made some time back when referring to Uncle Jim. While Tilly was a chatty and affectionate woman, apparently Jim was quiet, moody and stood no nonsense. Bill had once overheard Dad telling Mum of his temper. Apparently he had flogged one of the Aboriginal workers to straighten him out. He was pleased Kitty had not been listening in on that conversation. He wondered what it was like to live in Australia. Some of the orphans from England had been sent over there on an earlier boat. That one had left a week before theirs. They could just as easily have been on it as the one that brought them here to New Zealand.

CHAPTER 5

A thousand miles from New Zealand waves crashed against a reef that protected the barren Australian coast, and the turbulence became little more than a swell as it moved forward. There was hardly a ripple when it reached the shore. This was an area where salt-water crocodiles lurked in stagnant creeks, and only the very careful survived. Man or animal. Beyond the sand dunes, patches of vegetation had a precarious hold in the odd hollow, but the land soon gave way to desert. It was total desolation — a sun-scorched wasteland of bare rock and that all-engulfing sand. It stretched for miles, and for centuries prior to this had been home to the Aborigines. It was an unforgiving land for the unprepared. Natives in these parts survived mainly because of information passed down through countless generations — knowledge of plant and food cycles, and the natural habits of wildlife. Vegetation was mainly in the form of scrub, and somewhere out there amongst it all the Dwyers had their home and what remained of their stock.

Theirs was the only patch with drinkable water for hundreds of miles. A small community of Aboriginal workers and others. They all lived on Dwyer land in a collection of out-houses and lean-to's all clustered around the homestead. Jim Dwyer worked them hard, but they stayed anyway. It was a simple life. Work, eat, drink and sleep. Sometimes a bit of alcohol. There was no work elsewhere and nowhere to go. The next property was some one hundred and fifty miles to the south. Although Tilly had been ill for weeks, few visitors were expected. Distance put paid to that, and so they were restricted to radio contact once a day if lucky. Out here, Dwyer's word was law, and he took full advantage of his position of authority. He was head of the house, the boss and the biggest land holder for hundreds of miles. He had little regard for regulations, and did things simply because he could. No one ever questioned him. Not even Tilly.

This week Dwyer had men off fixing fences, and others were repairing roofs. The house, and just about every other building, required some attention. Things deteriorated quickly in the harsh climate. He sat back in the cool of the veranda and surveyed the ground around his homestead. Heat-haze shimmered in front of him. Two of the house-girls were painting a fence. It was probably was not necessary but he had to keep them occupied somehow. Paint was an expensive luxury, but both he and Tilly liked things as neat as possible. A coat of paint always freshened up the place and, in any event, they had the property on the market now. Anyone could fly in at any stage so it was best to keep things up to date. Paint freshened the buildings for a while, but few things stayed looking new for very long around here. Dwyer knew his wife barely tolerated the place, so these mundane tasks helped dress up the property to her liking and kept her happy. The girls were tittering as they went about their work, and Dwyer leaned forward to check them. They had been laughing about their elders going bush in search of witchetty grubs for tonight's dinner. These native teenagers were caught between the traditions of their people and the convenience foods of the twentieth century.

'Concentrate on what yer doing, you two gollies,' he said in a stern and insulting voice.

Quiet was restored. In fact, if it had not been for the buzzing of flies, there would have been no sound at all. He liked it this way, and tilted his hat forward so he could doze in a half-sleep for a while.

When the sun moved onto his face later, he rose and sauntered off down the path for a piddle behind a building. When he was done, he entered one of the sheds not far from the house and sat for a while in the cool. Most were locked for obvious reasons, but there was nothing of value in this one. Just a place to get out of the sun. Ten minutes or so passed before agitated voices attracted his attention. He moved to the door and pushed it open just a little. From the outside no one would have been aware of his presence. With only his eye to the crack he felt as confident as one of those 'crocs' he had hunted in the past. Hidden from view. Quiet. Waiting to pounce.

The girls were busy on hands and knees trying to disguise the spilt paint. One of them had apparently stepped back and up-ended the pail. While only a small amount had been lost, there was still a mess to clean. He watched them with narrowed eyes. It annoyed him, but at the same time he enjoyed their predicament. He smirked, searching their frightened faces as they attempted to hide the mistake. And then finally, after what seemed an age, Dwyer moved. Gliding silently up the path he paused, towering above them, saying nothing initially. Suddenly aware of his presence they both rose, and stood quietly with heads bowed. Both girls knew their place.

'Well?'

'Not me, boss,' said one quickly, turning slightly, and looking at the other. They were both in their late teens, although it was hard to tell. To some, Aboriginals were not the most attractive of races and their women seemed to age quickly. Often you could get no conversation at all from them. He found them sullen and shifty much of the time.

The older one said nothing, but it was clear to Jim that she had been the cause of the accident. He considered his options. Docking their meager pay was the least preferred. It only made for more bitterness, and usually led to vandalism or theft.

'Go wait by the supply shed,' he said at last. He may as well turn this situation to his advantage, he thought with a sneer.

With a knowing look she ambled off, slopping along, scuffing feet in that lazy manner that he detested so much. The other one finished off the 'clean-up', and Dwyer stood by to ensure both paintbrushes were done properly before dismissing her for the day. In the meantime other workers had finished repairs they had been assigned around the property, and moved on as arranged to help with a fencing job half an hour from the house.

Tilly was still asleep. Her medication kept her bedridden day in and day out. He could see her through the window, and decided not to disturb this 'quiet time' of hers. He would have a cup of tea ready for them both later. Half an hour passed before he headed for the shed. He had deliberately let her wait. The girl was standing in the shade, and rose out of respect as he approached. Nothing was said as he unlocked the padlock. There were no trusted employees around here. No half measures taken. Anything worth stealing had to be locked away. There were a number of sheds on the property, and this one had a mustiness about it. Lack of ventilation coupled with the smells that came from fuel and oil containers, old mattresses and discarded curtaining. There was one permanently closed window allowing some light in, but that was all. Unlike the other outhouse, this one was hotter inside than out. She followed him in, and he shut the door behind them.

'Waste my paint will you?'

'Very sorry boss.'

'Always mucking around instead of getting on with the job.'

'Yes boss, sorry boss.'

It was getting late in the afternoon but he took all the time he wanted. A breeze had started up outside, and the temperature would soon begin dropping.

Dwyer emerged from the shed a while later, scratching his crotch and adjusting his clothing as he walked away. He was perspiring and needed a drink. The girl had scurried away a minute or so earlier. This was the third time in as many weeks that he had 'punished' her. Usually he had to look for an excuse. Today she had brought it upon herself. Nothing was said, they simply went their separate ways.

Tilly woke to find her drink already prepared and beside her bed. Dwyer raised his voice so he could talk to her from the kitchen. He needed a shower before coming any closer to his wife.

'We've done a fair bit today, dear,' he said encouragingly. 'Fencing, some roofing, even a bit of fresh paintwork for you.'

'That's good,' she said weakly. I'm pleased for that.'

• • • • • • •

Sad news came later that month in the form of a letter from Jim. Bill watched as his Dad stood outside for a long time. He seemed to be reading and re-reading, almost in the hope the written words would change. His sister, Tilly, had died. None of them could believe it at first. They had all been aware of her occasional health problems, of course, but had no idea she had been so poorly for so long. Aunt Tilly had finally succumbed to an influenza epidemic that was rife in their area. The Dwyers had already agreed to an offer on their farm, and that deal would naturally proceed. He was expected on his own late in November.

'He'll arrive just after your birthdays.'

The Wilsons built up Bill and Kitty's expectations of Jim. The family would make this as good a visit as possible for him, and also for Dad. As the time drew nearer, thoughts of Aunt Tilly diminished, and both kids began to talk about stories he would bring of the wild Australian desert, man-eating crocodiles and terrifying convicts.

Dwyer's arrival in Sydney marked the end of the second stage of his journey. For him the whole exercise was a big undertaking, and he had mapped out in his mind five specific steps that would get him to his New Zealand destination. Of course the first had been a general clean-up and departure from the land he had farmed for many years. Although a hardened man, he found it sad to put all that behind him and simply walk away. And then there was Tilly's grave. He had sat beside the basic gravestone nestled there in the best part of her garden gathering his thoughts, and knowing he would never set foot on this piece of dirt again. Dwyer remembered the good times they had shared together, and those fond memories tugged at his heart.

Having successfully transported his belongings this far to the Sydney waterfront, and having now arranged suitable storage until the end of the month, he faced a delay of two or three weeks before departure. He was rather looking forward to the voyage across the Tasman Sea to Wellington. This current gap in his travel arrangements was a planned one though. Dwyer needed a breather, so the third stage was welcome relief now he had his gear off his hands. The fourth and fifth steps would be the voyage to New Zealand and train trip to family. After that, he thought he might just explore his new country before making any further plans. In the meantime he was here and keen to make the most of it, so his decision to carry on south to the Gippsland area and check out one of the national parks was a good way of filling in time. He had heard of the place from a worker passing through his property years ago. Someone who had stayed a month doing casual work, and whose only conversation, when there had been time to talk, was of the splendour and history of the park.

'Great place if you want to get away from it all, mate. They used to train our commandos down there during the war. In fact, the visitor's centre where you can arrange accommodation today used to be part of their barracks and kitchen block.' In his mind he could still hear the bloke's voice describing the area.

Everything had fallen into place rather well so far, but he was not at all happy in the 'big smoke', and his desire to escape to a quieter refuge showed in his frown lines. A fortunate conversation in a bar later that day resulted in his departing Sydney's city limits in the comfort of a furniture delivery truck heading to places south. Although happy to take the free lift, he contributed little to the conversation, effectively depriving the driver of any companionship the man might have been looking for. When awake, his 'yes' and 'no' answers brought about an uncomfortable silence between them. It was hardly surprising, therefore, that his lift ran out at a fuel stop some seven hours into the trip following a brief and sharp exchange of words. He had been lucky to have travelled as far as that. Dwyer cared not that he had been left to find his own way from that point on, pleased only that he had come hundreds of miles and covered a good portion of the intended distance. A lingering salty smell of the coast teased his nostrils, as he shouldered his pack and headed on. Not much later, a sign indicating a camping ground some five miles further down the road determined his destination for the night.

Four days had passed since the truck incident. He had bunked down in a cooking shelter for a couple of days before being ordered out of the caravan park for staying without arrangement, or payment, and had successfully thumbed a number of lifts, putting even more mileage behind him. Wilson's Prom had been a haven for walkers since its conversion to national park status in the early 1900s. Its numerous pathways through boulder-strewn forests enabled people to enjoy its solitude, and yet the park was only a couple of hours from Melbourne city. Numerous huts at the park headquarters were available, as were caravan and tent sites. Very structured and clean, it was the attraction of the area, with its mix of dry and rain forests together with its safe swimming beaches, and it brought thousands each weekend to experience a bit of untouched Australia. Dwyer was pleased he was here mid-week when other visitors were few and far between. He was also pleased to have the trip down through Nowra, Batemans Bay and Narooma behind him. An overnight break at Merimbula had been worth the stop, but it was unlikely he would do the trip again. He had quickly grown sick of the relentless shimmering heat on the road stretching beyond them. Tar seal bordered by clay banks and undergrowth just waiting for a careless match to set it all alight.

He squatted now on a rocky granite outcrop far from one of the small car parks, and studied the extent of the valley below. Thousands of trees, and probably an equal number of house-sized boulders, lay before him. There was still evidence of the severe fire that had torn through a portion of the land back in 1951. Trees some sixty metres in height, and with impressive circumferences, had somehow missed earlier logging efforts only to perish in that inferno. The now rotting remains dotted amongst undergrowth proved previous existence to those able to look beyond the mass of smaller bluegum, mountain ash and yellow stringy bark varieties that had quickly replaced them in sheltered gullies and on upper slopes.

The track he had been following zigzagged back and forth below his vantage point, and in one part branched to the left, giving less enthusiastic trampers an easier route back to their vehicles. Coming into view now was a woman. Alone, and lightly dressed, she strode along at a brisk pace, seemingly disinterested in the beauty surrounding her. She was still a good way off, and he wondered whether others were spread out behind her. Certainly the few he had already encountered today had been in small groups. He needed only wait a moment before he had his answer. Her initial pace slowed as the track steepened, and at the junction she paused, uncertain as to which was the correct option. She waited, bent double catching her breath, and at times looking back down the path as if expecting someone to catch up. Eventually two men came into view, and although Dwyer could clearly see them, the companions were still out of her sight and some minutes away from the division in the track. Keen to get on, he watched as she scratched an arrow in the dirt indicating the path to take and set off again. Within seconds she was lost from view in a tree-filled gully, but heading uphill in his direction. When the men reached the junction they were so busy conversing with each other, the sign she had left went unnoticed as they chose the easier gradient to the left and moved away in the opposite direction.

Dwyer rose from his spot, mind racing. Ever the opportunist, he quickly planned his moves and stepped back onto the main track to wait. With head down, and positioning each step carefully on the rough rising ground ahead of her, the advancing woman was not at all conscious of his presence. His eyes drilled into her, mentally undressing her. He knew from experience that in those last few steps she would finally sense his presence. He had seen it happen with animals, and knew it was imperative not to make eye contact until the last possible second. Not this time however. He was willing her to look at him. It was a game, and he was enjoying every moment of it.

Her head jerked up and their eyes met.

'My God, you gave me a start,' she gasped aloud, straightening, looking about, suddenly uncertain of her safety.

Realising she would view his leering smirk as a threat he bowed his head a little, stepped back a pace, and changed his smile slightly. Just enough to give some measure of reassurance.

'Sorry Miss, only waiting for my wife,' he lied. 'She's taking photos over there.'

Dwyer pointed back to the rock promontory, and briefly described the fantastic view. Already the woman's body language had changed from that of vulnerability to a display of relief.

'Go and have a look. You'll be able to see any others who may be on the track too.'

He stepped aside, hanging back a moment, giving her both the freedom to pass him and the choice to look for herself. It was only a matter of six or eight paces to the edge. And the drop was not a sheer one, more a long slope down some rough ground.

'Tell my wife it's time we got on our way,' he called, continuing the bluff.

'I can't see her,' came the reply after a bit of a pause.

Dwyer mumbled something audibly about the length of time photographers take, and headed unthreateningly towards the woman.

'Let me have a look,' he said, with a sound of frustration in his voice.

• • • • • • •

From five yards off it was obviously a campsite of sorts. But looking back from beyond that distance, the sun-faded yellow and green awning blended perfectly into its surroundings. Dwyer had thought of this earlier in the week when making his selection from unoccupied caravans. He needed something about that size for protection from the elements, and felt the canvas cover would make a useful fly. In this heat a fly as opposed to an airless tent was a necessity, and he had stretched the cover out in the form of a roof, but a couple of feet off the ground at its two lower edges. It served the role admirably. He saw no advantage in advertising his presence to others, so privacy through camouflage had also been a consideration.

It was time to move on, and although a clear patch would remain for a while before the natural fall of leaves obliterated any sign of his camp, he was not too concerned. Normally he would have kicked the pile of leaves originally swept to one side back over the flattened area to disguise any evidence of his presence, and also to hide the scar left by his fire. No point this time. It was unlikely others would venture this far off the track for a while, and besides the hump of leaves served a more important purpose at the moment.

She had cooperated completely. Too fearful to do otherwise two days ago when he had flicked open the knife, grabbed her roughly by the upper arm, and growled instructions menacingly. It had happened so quickly, and before she had had time to react in any way whatsoever, he had manhandled her over the lip and down the slope. Within seconds they had moved far from the track, travelling quickly through undergrowth that had torn at both bodies as they ran. While trying to fall, to collapse her legs and hinder progress he had somehow kept her upright and moving forward. His power and the ever-present weapon kept her silent, and she had the sense to remain so later, even when it had became obvious he was going to gag her with his dirty handkerchief. Just in case.

On arrival at the campsite he had given her a few hard slaps, in case she had any silly thoughts he was not a serious threat. It would ensure her continued cooperation, he decided. And then he tied her in such a way as to leave his victim completely helpless. It was a technique he had found effective in the past. Elbow to elbow, but loosely across the back. Enough slack to hinder any acrobatic movements, finishing with each wrist secured to the appropriate ankle. He left her for an hour like that, going off to ensure there were no telltale signs left back on the track. Shouts way off in the distance were obviously from those out looking for the missing woman. But they were too far away to worry him. Even so, he realised he would have to have a small smokeless fire for the next few nights. He had the skill to do that, minimising any chance of detection. Returning later it did not surprise him to find her in the same position. He knew it was near-impossible for her to move, and he ignored her discomfort, knowing that in time she would have no feeling left in her limbs and would be completely at his mercy.

Dwyer began talking to her in a normal manner as if their very existence in this isolation was nothing out of the ordinary, not expecting any answer of course. No response was possible beyond a pleading look with the eyes. A look that later turned to silent horror when he began cutting and removing clothing in his efforts to more thoroughly examine his catch.

His departure from the park took place during the night, and while wanting to be well away from the area before accepting his first lift, he took his time this evening. In a way Dwyer felt trapped. Too much open country for his liking and a cloudless night of all things. The moon eventually made itself apparent. Emerging at last from behind coastal hills and bathing the land with a soft amber light. Everything was lit up, accounting for his earlier uneasiness at the prospect of being out on the road. He had been used to the odd quick exit in his youth when on the run, but around here what little there was in the way of vegetation worried him. Standing every chance of being detected if a fast vehicle approached, a more cautious strategy was appropriate this time, and he found a comfy spot on the upper slopes of something known locally as Big Hummock and waited for a change in the weather. His map showed this was one of two sets of dunes affording an unrestricted view of the surrounding countryside, and an ideal place to sit out his wait. Low clouds finally rolled inland in the small hours of the morning, silently approaching then completely blocking the moonlight. Dwyer set off across the Yanakie Isthmus, a sandy bar connecting the promontory with the mainland. With the gloom as protection his confidence increased, and he felt better in the cooler breeze. It was easier going now. The land, flattened through seasonal grazing over this past hundred years, boasted an abundance of wildlife including grey kangaroos and the wary emu. Nothing was seen tonight, however, and no one saw him.

Many hours later when the opportunity finally arrived, he willingly accepted a ride. This time it was an unusually talkative Dwyer who entertained the driver with stories about the farm he had left behind and his plans for the future.

'Wife died a while back, so had to sell it off. Some lucky bugger's got it now. Best bit of dirt in that area and had to let it go for a song.'

'You looking for something down this way then?'

'Nah. Couldn't match it mate. Nothing around here worth my money. Nah, I'm off to see family for a spell then probably travel the world. Bit of work here and there. Don't expect to stay long in New Zealand anyway. Sheep aren't my thing, and besides the country's too small. I'm used to 'big' mate, and you don't get much bigger than what I've left behind.'

'You'll be considering the States then?'

'Not bloody likely, mate. They're all mad up there in the USA,' Dwyer replied scathingly. 'Read an article once about some character in his thirties who'd killed his parents then asked the court for leniency on the grounds he was an orphan. How in the hell do you explain that sort of carry on?'

With the coming of dawn it was clearly going to be another hot day. There had been no sharing of the driving, so Dwyer had been able to doze on and off between conversations. In those few quiet moments when it seemed there was nothing left to talk about, his private thoughts returned to activities over recent days at the campsite. He smirked as he thought of what he had been doing repetitively throughout that first night with her, and indeed well on into the following morning. He had left the site for half a day, only to return to resume his lurid activities when no searchers entered their section of the park. It had been easy despatching her, and he wondered how many flies would now be investigating the contents of that mound of leaves. But as quickly as the look of pleasure crossed his face, it also drained away as memories were recalled of the past decade. It felt to him like a life-time of rejection. A hard climate for a woman, of course, and his wife had not coped well with their rustic way of life, with limited water and an absence of those generally accepted niceties of life. Despite her loneliness, and a craving for companionship, she eventually restricted him to a reluctant 'once a monther', and it was little wonder he sought his pleasure elsewhere. Naturally any girls on the property became the focus of his attention, either as willing or resisting recipients of his advances, but also as he satisfied his perverted needs by dishing out inappropriate punishments. And this latest episode in the park had been a real battle. He was now looking for something better. Someone willing would be good. And younger too.

'Sydney's not far off.'

The driver's voice brought him back to his senses, and he focused his thoughts on those arrangements he had ahead of him. It was then, and only then, that he came to the realisation he was finally free to travel at will. Until now, the full effect of the sale of his property had not really sunk in. An immense burden had in effect been taken from him, and at last he could look forward to his departure from Sydney with enthusiasm.

CHAPTER 6

They had been waiting for ages, but Jim Dwyer finally arrived at Woodside railway station on the Auckland train from Wellington. A lot had happened during the past months. His brother-in-law and young Bill were standing on the platform when the carriages ground to a halt, and the twosome gave him the warmest of welcomes.

'God, you look fit, man. Welcome to the Wairarapa.'

It was not exactly a truthful comment, for during the past two weeks he had used bus, ship and train. While it had been a good enough journey, Dwyer was sick of travel, and this was clearly evident in the tired, drawn look on his face.

'Fit? Hell's bells, mate, I feel bloody exhausted,' he replied, making no allowance for others within earshot of his colourful language.

Bill stood nearby smiling, and was quite taken by his uncle's ginger moustache. Same colour as his own hair, but in Dwyer's case caused by years of cigarette smoke.

Tall, wiry, with a weary smile and rumpled travelling clothes, he seemed friendly enough. So much so that Bill cast aside any thoughts this was the same tough man he had heard would whip his workers without hesitation. Perhaps the original teller of the tale had stretched the truth.

'You've got so much luggage,' Dad laughed after the initial greeting and some brief talk about Aunt Tilly's death. 'We'll drop you off home and come back for the rest. It'll be no problem, but let's try to get it all in anyway.'

It was not long before they left the tar seal. The gravelled section was the slow bit.

'Something wrong with the car?'

'What do you mean?'

'Well where I come from it's foot to the boards, and just let her go.'

'I guess,' Wilson replied with a smile, 'you're used to long stretches of traffic-free roading, and as straight as an arrow too. Over here we have to cater for Kitty when she's with us. She doesn't travel well on these windy bits, and I've simply become used to taking it easily. Besides, this is a bit of an old girl we've got here, and I prefer to nurse her along and avoid the repair bills.'

They ended up having to make the two trips after all. Uncle Jim moved into Bill's bedroom, and he got to sleep on the living room couch which was a novelty. Both kids warmed to him right from the start. Like their Mum and Dad, he too had time to play and tell countless stories, keeping them entertained for hours. Uncle Jim cut stacks of firewood ready for next winter and took a liking for the push mower. Had no need for a lawnmower where he had come from. The grass around the Wilson's home had never looked so good, and the whole property took on a new look of neatness and orderliness. Although Dwyer had been used to having staff do cleaning for him, he was prepared to roll up his sleeves in order to keep the place shipshape. That preference to have things straight and tidy eventually rubbed off on Bill who quickly adopted the same standards.

'I just can't get over the fact you have so few flies. They sit all over your face back in Oz.'

Everything was 'back in Oz' for a while.

He had another expression they found funny too. Whenever Uncle Jim was really sure of his facts, he'd say, 'Ten bob to a knob of that other stuff.' The kids had no idea what he was referring to, but the saying amused them.

Although rural, the family relied on town supply for their milk. Others in the area invariably had a house cow. The Wilson's supply arrived daily with Mr Johnston, their postie, and it came in glass bottles with his mail. Until now they had got by on a quart a day, but with Uncle Jim's arrival the order was upped by an extra pint. If you were careful not to shake the bottle, you could gently pour off the cream that accumulated at the top, and Kitty showed him how to do it at breakfast.

'Most people just give it a good shake to mix it back in, but we love the cream on Mum's porridge,' Kitty explained.

With no fridge they had always got on okay with their cool-air-safe hanging off the side of the house. One evening, however, the sausages must have been in the sun a bit too long at some stage and were not the best.

'I'm not too sure about these snarlers.' Uncle Jim had all these strange words and expressions.

Mum thought they smelled a bit suspect during the cooking. A bit suspect maybe, but you simply did not throw away food on a whim. Not in these parts. First bite though, and the message was clear.

'Definitely off. You'd better have a word with your butcher, mate,' Uncle Jim said.

Then as an aside. 'Makes them himself does he, mate? With horse-cock and sawdust by the taste.'

They both fell about laughing while Mum got all flustered and scolded them. They were being coarse, and were eventually shooed off outside for a fag while the kids found themselves being organised with evening dishes. As the men walked towards the door, Jim started to recite a poem.

Scabby ol sausages
really hurt my Tum
Sore holes, big Moles,
and pimples on my Bum

'Time for bed you two,' she told the kids, 'especially if the men are going to talk like that. Bill, you can bunk down in our room until your couch is free.'

He was not going to complain. It was fun having Uncle Jim there and good to see everyone so happy.

'I want to stay up longer,' said Kitty. 'Uncle Jim can tell us more stories.'

Dwyer hesitated at the door and looked back at her disapprovingly. He waited for an appropriate reprimand from the Wilsons which did not eventuate. It simply confirmed earlier thoughts he had that she was a bit lippy at times, and that the Wilsons were too weak. Tonight he said nothing. Basically the kids were okay. Perhaps overly tired after the activities of the day. 'Ten bob to a knob of that other stuff,' he thought to himself, 'the day will come and she will get her come-uppance.'

It was a time of learning for both kids. One night he took them for a walk by torchlight down to the stream.

'You may have been down here many times during the day, you two, but wait until you see what it's like at night.'

When everyone was ready he switched off the torch. In the damp recesses of the clay bank a whole new world emerged. Glow worms everywhere. Kitty and Bill tried to get the glowing lights onto their fingers, without success. On another occasion they rose at 6.00 a.m., and set off with packed lunches. This time just the three of them. The drive took about half an hour and they chatted happily. Uncle Jim was interested in what they had been up to over the years, just about as much as they were in the stories he had to tell. A suitable spot was found and they left the car beside the road.

'It'll be okay here. Come on, race you to the river.'

He led the way, following a gurgling stream which eventually led to the Ruamahanga river. It was one of many larger flows of water to emerge from high ground behind farmland, only to lose pace as it weaved its way across the flats towards the coast. There were plenty of places to have lunch but the mosquitos were hell. Great black clouds of them. They eventually found their way out onto a shingle bed and had lunch there in the middle. It was pleasant sitting on a stranded log, its now unmoving hulk no doubt washed down in a previous flood. They used its sun-bleached surface as both a seat and a table. Both kids already knew how to skip stones across water, so that was something Uncle Jim was unable to teach them. But he was able to instruct them on how to do a piercing whistle using two fingers in the mouth, and it was a couple of excited children who, having mastered the technique, longed to get home to show their parents.

Some canoeists drifted past, appearing so quietly they gave Kitty a bit of a start. Three doubles and a single.

'It must be really great to travel so swiftly and silently like that. To explore the river and find out what's around the next bend,' said Bill. 'Perhaps one day I'll have a canoe of my own.'

It was a good outing but the car was a long way off, and by mid-afternoon they needed to get on their way again before the sun dropped below the ridge.

Jim was a good friend and had lots of time for them. He was instrumental in their having a real wetting one sunny afternoon. A real 'shorts and singlet' day it was, and although still officially winter, it was not uncommon for the area to sometimes experience a summery day. With an old tarpaulin as a liner in a discarded tractor tyre, they soon had the makings of a small pool. With plenty of tank water on hand, they filled the tyre and were soon splashing each other and having a right rowdy time. Thoroughly wet through, scantily clad but not feeling at all uncomfortable, the kids paraded back and forth doing their best to soak each other. All three adults sat and watched from the shade of the veranda, with the Wilsons laughing heartily at the youngsters' enjoyment. Dwyer watched with more of a leer than a laugh, quietly drinking in the scene.

He was knowledgeable too. If the car ever required attention, it was no problem to him. He helped his brother-in-law fix one or two things on a job where a bit of extra muscle was needed, and during those first few weeks a lot of awkward chores that had previously been conveniently put to one side were finished. It was while working together one day that he suggested they get away for a bit and leave him to mind the kids.

'Take a week off and head up north, you two,' he said again that night. 'Do it while you've got the chance. I'll cover the cost. There wasn't much left over from the farm after the solicitor and bank got their hooks on what they were owed, you know. But all that aside, I've got a bit there, and you're welcome to a trip away on me.'

It was a truly generous offer, and it took only a moment for a decision to be made.

'Uncle Jim's going to look after you two for a wee while,' their mother said. 'Your father and I will have a few days, maybe a week, up in Rotorua.'

'Can't we come too?' they chorused, without thinking of their uncle's feelings.

The family had often talked about a trip to the thermal area, but in the past there had been neither the time nor the money. There was a bit of a discussion, but finally it was agreed the kids would have to wait for another time. The Wilsons left that following Sunday with Bill and Kitty chasing them down the driveway as far as the letterbox. With lots of laughter and waving they left in a cloud of dust and headed off down the road. And then they had gone.

'So what shall we do today, you two? How about we build a flying fox?' he continued without waiting for a response.

'What's that?'

There were genuine looks of interest on their faces as their uncle explained how he could stretch a rope from one of the bigger trees to the base of another right across their back yard.

'Then we attach that pulley I've seen around here somewhere, add a seat to it, and that's a flying fox. You just climb up the tree, hop on, and ride down the cable to the end.'

'Sounds scary,' said Kitty, not really convinced she would give it a go.

'It'll be as safe as anything,' he laughed. 'You'll see. Ten bob to a knob of that other stuff you'll be back up there for another go.'

'Sounds great,' said Bill, who thought it would be just the thing for him, Ben and Abel. 'We could build a hut up there and have the cable coming from that.'

It was as if the family was jinxed. Both kids arrived home from school two days later to find a police car at the house, and were immediately aware of an unusual silence about the place. Uncle Jim walked towards them, his ashen face indicating all was not right. No one could imagine how awkward he felt about having police on the property, but that discomfort was easily disguised by his reaction to the dreadful news they had delivered. When he sat the kids down on a stump, and squatted before them, they could see he was very upset.

'I'm so sorry, you two.'

He hesitated, looking away unable to make eye contact or to pick the right words it seemed.

'We have some shocking news.'

He told how their parents had made an early start from a small town called Levin, and chosen to take the national park route north to Taupo and on to Rotorua. At mid-day there had been a car crash. No one else was involved. They had simply missed a bridge and gone straight into the river.

'Are they okay?'

'No Kitty. I'm sorry... They're... dead. It's icy water straight from Mt Ruapehu's crater lake. They didn't stand a chance, and drowned before anyone could reach them.'

There were always going to be lots of questions, but for now the tears flowed from all three as the shock set in. It seemed unbelievable that such a short time ago they had lost Aunt Tilly, and now this.

'It's terrible, I know. Don't worry too much though, I'm here to look after and protect you,' he said crouching there with a 'fatherly' arm around each of them. 'I'll help you both through this ordeal. It'll be all right, you'll see. I promise it'll be okay.'

'I'm their only family,' he explained again to the nearest constable. 'Best just leave us to it, eh? Oh, and thanks for taking over the arrangements and all that.'

Christmas was going to be a quiet affair for the trio. There had not been a lot to organise. The funeral service had been taken off their hands and had just come and gone. It was more a matter of getting on with things despite the great emptiness that existed. Some weeks later in the same spot at Tangiwai, the Wangaehu river claimed the lives of many others, marking the spot as the country's worst rail disaster. Miles away, and high up the slopes, a mud-slide had rumbled its way down, following the stream and then the river. Residents of nearby Waiouru had heard, but ignored, the deep grumbling voice of the mountain. Like an inland tidal wave, it had surged onward sweeping all before it until finally a seemingly robust rail bridge was its last major obstacle. Steam engine KA 949 was heading for Auckland, hauling almost a dozen heavy carriages. It pressed on at a steadily growing pace with its driver unaware of any danger ahead, thundering forward until those very last seconds when a desperate effort was made to arrest its momentum. But the tracks had simply disappeared, and with a horrendous crash everything was consumed by the raging torrent. It was much the same spot as the Wilson accident just a few weeks earlier.

This latest tragedy made the news in a big way. All newspapers followed the incident, and had numerous articles about the crash site. There was a photograph of a railway employee pointing out the crushed and wrecked carriages to the Prime Minister, Mr Holland, as they stood on the riverbank staring at foaming water and cruel, slate-grey rocks. It came out later that the bridge had been weakened back in 1925 but never properly repaired. Daily lists of the dead featured in the papers as bodies were recovered. By comparison, their parents' deaths had almost gone unnoticed.

Uncle Jim was kind enough to let them miss the first days of the new school year. It had now been many weeks of sunshine, but the summer break had hardly been the same this time. The weeks had dragged on slowly, leaving periods where they were unable to remember where the time had gone or what they had been doing. But eventually they had to go back to school, if for no other reason but to re-establish some routine again.

There had been many visitors. Scones and containers of soup appeared mysteriously on the doorstep, and the flow of concerned locals was endless. Things quietened down eventually, and they all did their best to get on with their lives. There were some funny moments amongst it all that helped create the odd smile. When someone brought a cake for example. They hardly knew the woman, but thought her name was Mrs Smith. It did not matter. She had always been regarded locally as being a cake baker of note. Had been well thought of for many years. At some stage, however, a load of suspect flour had been delivered. She had probably been buying it by the barrel, and it had become damp or gone off. Clearly she was oblivious to this fact, and no one had had the heart to tell her. In any event her baking suffered as a result, and the threesome received several bad cakes during the period, each one as horrible, if not worse, than the one before. It got to the stage where no sooner had the offending cake been delivered to their door, than it was broken into bits and heaved onto the back lawn for the poor birds to dispose of. During one incident Uncle Jim was on hands and knees scrabbling about retrieving the pieces. They had accepted the cake graciously and sent her on her way, but had luckily noticed her returning ten minutes or so later and had been able to react just in time.

'Forgot to take my tin. Enjoy the baking. It's one of my best.'

Afterwards they laughed and giggled at nearly being caught out, and in any event they had probably done the birds a great service. Perhaps it was just a way of releasing the tension. A happier moment for once, but still unlike the good old days.

The accident had affected Dwyer as well. He now had responsibilities he had not been prepared for. He spent long periods just thinking. The kids also wondered about their future, and how he felt about being lumbered with them. Would he return to Australia without them? They had no idea. To be left stranded with absolutely no one was too frightening a thing to consider. Uncle Jim's standards started to slip. His rough stubble, half-bearded appearance indicated a man who not only had no wife to consider, but who also envisaged a bleak future ahead of him. The constantly sunny days helped to some extent, and at first there was little change in their lifestyle or daily routine. Each day started as the one before. Chooks fed at 5.00 a.m. and eggs, if any, collected. Kitty and Bill alternated day about with that chore. Even in summer there was a need for a plentiful supply of firewood as the wood stove still had to be fed. That was Bill's job. The amount of effort he put into the task determined whether he could go a whole week before another period of chopping and stacking, or whether it was reduced to a daily chore. A regular ritual, however, was the shifting of smaller amounts from the woodshed to the wood box outside the kitchen door. There was always a need for dry kindling to get a healthy fire going. Jim did most of the cooking. General tidiness within the house was Kitty's domain, and she accompanied her uncle to the shops once a fortnight to help get groceries and any other requirements. She hated those trips. Bill decided it was probably because of the way he drove along that dusty, windy road. Kitty had always been a bad traveller and remained quiet for days afterwards. He was pleased car sickness was not a problem for him.

At the start of February, Jim was asked if he would take the vacant position at the mill. The work would be heavy, and the hours long, but with three mouths to feed what else could he do? He felt obliged to accept the offer, despite the fact he still had some money hidden away. It was only a little, and needed to last as he had no real idea of what the future held for him.

'Bloody rogues,' he'd mutter to himself every time he thought of those legal costs and associated deductions from the sale price in order to wipe his loans. Apart from anything else, it was his emergency fund if he ever needed to get back to Australia in a hurry. He was determined to leave it untouched meantime.

Each evening he returned tired and hungry. The kids noticed changes in him, and sometimes there was an uncomfortable atmosphere in the house. Mostly he had little to say to them anyway, and no interest whatsoever in their achievements at school. As the weeks passed he became less involved in the day-to-day running of the home, but frequently found fault with their efforts around the place. He seemed to look for things to pick on.

'For heavens sake, Bill, will you sit up properly at the table. And you Kitty, I haven't cooked that for nothing you know. I expect it all eaten.'

Then there would be further periods of silence, and sometimes he threatened to straighten them out if they continued to displease him. Both kids were frightened when he spoke that way.

And yet, there were occasions when their uncle represented everything they needed. Mr Wilson had taught Bill how to hunt when the kids first arrived in New Zealand, and now some time later Dwyer found time to carry on the tuition. These were the moments Bill enjoyed most, and it was easy to dismiss any other periods of rough gruffness as perhaps being something he or Kitty had caused. When his uncle gave him the special attention he was obviously crying out for, Bill was at his happiest. Dwyer had quickly adapted to the New Zealand bush and animals, soon realising his Australian outback skills were just as relevant over here.

'Frightened deer always run uphill if they can, and pigs generally head down, making their own track. Best you get well out of the way if a pig is charging downhill, Bill.'

He also showed the boy how to make a fire in the wet, and where best to doss down if ever caught out overnight. Bill absorbed everything like a sponge, knowing Uncle Jim's teachings were based on experience.

'You'll not learn stuff like this from a book you know. You've got to get out there and do it.'

Dwyer paused for a moment before adding, 'You can forget all that boy scout crap too. Rubbing sticks together is rubbish. You want a fire in the bush, then you'll need a candle. Something to keep the flame going. A candle, a knife and a bit of patience will do it every time.'

'I'll show you another fire trick too. Go get my torch and that box of Steelos.'

Kitty ran for the Steelos under the kitchen bench. The wire wool pads were good for cleaning pots, but she could not imagine how you could light a fire with them. Uncle Jim sat them down in front of him, and lined up the torch batteries in a groove where the veranda boards met. He carefully stretched the steel wool out so it was much the same thickness throughout, and long enough so it could link the positive and negative terminals.

'Before we start, check your pockets. I want any dry bits of lint and fluff you've got. When we put it all together, we might only have a few seconds to get it right, so you have to really prepare yourself properly for this if you want to get it burning. Best done by two people, this.'

Bill took the hint and held everything together, ensuring the strip of steel wool was firmly in touch with the two ends of the line of batteries. Uncle Jim concentrated on the middle section of steel wool. He gently teased it out until only a few strands were left. All heads were within inches of the other as they crouched over the apparatus. Jim introduced the tinder material to the fuse-like portion which was glowing faintly. They could smell the heat of the wire, even feel the warmth, but on this occasion the fluff did not ignite.

'Never mind, I know it works,' Uncle Jim announced after a while. 'May be we haven't got enough oomph in our batteries. Next time I've got the rifle out, I'll show you an even cleverer way to start a fire,' he promised.

Dwyer even made the effort to turn up at the school sports day. Aware that young Bill had been training hard for his cross-country event, he found himself shoulder to shoulder with other parents egging on the kids as they came into the home stretch. Earlier he had taken the boy aside for a few words of advice.

'I've never been a runner myself, Bill, but one thing I can tell you is this. It's not an all out sprint from the start. With five miles ahead of you, don't get too concerned if others charge off in front of the pack right from the beginning. Keep to the pace you're comfortable with, and then start to draw them in one at a time. If you find yourself up amongst the leaders, just hang back a bit boy. Always remember it's easier to be the hunter than the hunted. You'll see opportunities ahead of you in the last section of the run that they won't. I'm damn sure I wouldn't want to be leading a race and forever looking back over my shoulder.'

When it was over, Bill had finished well behind the winner. He felt really good though, and as a result of his uncle's advice had made up a lot of ground on the so-called better runners.

He found himself inwardly chanting 'easier-to-be-the-hunter-than-the hunted', 'easier-to-be-the-hunter-than-the hunted' throughout the race, and as a consequence had maintained a good rhythmic pace.

More often than not on Friday or Saturday nights, Uncle Jim would go bush, often borrowing Holloway's two dogs with which he had developed a special affinity. He was a skilled stalker, that was never in dispute, and a deer or a goat would keep them in meat for weeks. The only reason he was often unsuccessful with his hunting was because the area had been well cleaned out by 'government cullers' half a decade earlier. The animals existed, but were few and far between, and pretty flighty too. Nevertheless, he enjoyed stalking and giving tips to inexperienced people, whether they wanted the information or not.

'Always take a jacket, Bill,' he'd say. 'That's your most important piece of clothing. Covers your body's engine, if you know what I mean. Your important bits, understand? That's why you've got ribs too. Protection for your heart and lungs. If you've only got a jacket covering those organs then you'll survive longer than if you had good clothing elsewhere on your body. I'd rather be buck-naked and have a warm jacket, than be caught out with boots, trousers and a light shirt. You mark my words, boy, many a man has perished for want of a good jacket, having been caught out overnight.'

Bill hung on every word when Uncle Jim was talking like this. He had become the father figure that he needed in his life. Strange how instructions from those who had your respect stick with you. From that day on, Bill adopted a strict procedure from which he never strayed. Standing in the cold each morning, he would strip off his pyjamas, and from the pile lying on the floor there was a choice of any article of clothing to start with. But with Uncle Jim's comments in mind he always hunted out a singlet and shirt and got those on first. He was covering up and keeping his vital organs warm, acting as if restricted to the option of only being able to select one or two garments. In the years ahead he would find himself thinking of Jim Dwyer's words almost every time he got dressed.

One evening Uncle Jim entertained them with a trick he had learned as a young man. He had been preparing the usual billy tea they all enjoyed drinking before retiring for the night.

'You know how we have a boil up and throw in a handful of tea leaves? And how we then tap away at the side of the billy to make the floating leaves settle?' he asked them. 'Well the way we do it back home in Oz is like this.'

Dwyer took the bubbling billy from their stove and waited a moment for the steam to clear. With a measured handful of Choysa tea thown in, he explained a better method of settling the leaves.

'Centrifugal force,' he announced, pausing for effect.

Neither of the kids had any idea what he was on about, so he went on to explain how swinging the billy by its handle would have the same effect as 'tapping', and that the tea leaves would be forced to the bottom.

'I can do it without spilling a drop,' he claimed with confidence.

Bill and Kitty sought refuge by the couch as Uncle Jim checked ceiling height, and then positioned himself with plenty of room around him. Gripping the wire handle, he began to swing it back and forth, gently building higher and higher, and finally bringing it over in three full circles without any of the scalding contents falling. That was, until the handle gave way. Their shrieks of laughter must have been heard for miles.

But it was not always a happy home, and sometimes Bill and Kitty cherished those evenings when left alone. Usually he stayed out all night, and on these occasions they would stoke up the fire and doze the evening away on the couch. There was some comfort just lying there, listening to night noises the other side of a locked door. Usually opossums arguing with territorial cats. Almost all the cats were strays, and right from the start the kids had been told never to touch the disease-ridden animals. Battles at night were frequent and furious. On those rare opportunities when cats were seen during the day, it was of no surprise to anyone that they sported torn ears and bloody scratches.

CHAPTER 7

It was a time in their lives they were unlikely to forget and was to lead to many sleepless nights. Term one at school was now well underway, and what with daily chores and the period spent travelling to and from school, there was precious little time for play. Sometimes the hours after school passed too quickly. It was then a mad rush to get home before the deadline their uncle had set, and this was usually because they had stayed too long at the creek or chatting at a neighbour's gate.

The stove was lit every morning, supplying not only a means for cooking, but also heat for the antiquated hot water system and warmth for the house. It was not economic to keep it going all day by loading up and damping the flames down, so they simply let the fire die out, and usually it was easy enough to start afresh after school, aided by any remaining hot coals. Bill was generally good at having everything ready for when he arrived home. He had a healthy supply of kindling and dry bark, because to try using wood that was still 'green' was frustratingly difficult.

For some time now, Jim had been uncomfortable with the thought of any idle after-school activities the kids may have been pursuing. He had an inkling they were spending too much time playing when there were chores to attend to, and was keen for an opportunity to catch them out. When the mill closed early one afternoon, it gave him the chance to spend extra hours in the pub. But on this occasion, for one reason or another, the idea held little appeal, and he headed home driving past their gate and parking further up the road. It took only a few minutes to walk back across the paddocks to the rear of the house. There was no one at home when he arrived.

He could tell in advance because there was wood to cut, and he had been listening for the telltale sound of chopping. Dwyer headed for the 'Weta Shed'.

The kids arrived half an hour later, ambling along, then skylarking around the garden as usual, with no idea at all they were being watched. Bill finally fiddled around looking for scraps of dry kindling. His supply had been exhausted earlier in the week than expected, and today he was restricted to using mostly green stuff. He wished he had more time to work with this fire, as his uncle always expected to be able to start cooking as soon as he walked into the house. Kitty came outside to help, and was sent off to hunt around the sheds for better stuff, returning soon after with little in the way of dry material to contribute.

'It's starting to rain again,' she announced scurrying back inside.

Jim had seen enough, and dashed across the yard jumping puddles forming on the lawn. His frame filled the doorway, and he paused there, unseen by either child. Both were doing their best with the stove, but it simply would not work. Bill prodded the smouldering embers, and tried once more to blow a reluctant flame back into life.

'Stupid fire,' he muttered aloud, still not aware of his uncle's presence.

'We should have come home earlier, Kitty, and sorted out some better wood. If it doesn't go this time, I don't know what I'll do.'

Kitty had done her best to help but the yard had been picked clean of any small stuff over the past few days, and besides she had other duties. With little chance to tidy up the living area, their breakfast things were still scattered about the bench in an untidy pile. A living room full of smoke and mess from the morning gave a clear message to their uncle, and his raised voice made them both jump with surprise.

'You bloody idle brats. This place is a tip. Late home again, and look at that fire. Useless, both of you.'

'It's not our fault,' Kitty was quick to retaliate. 'It's the wood. It's too wet.'

For a moment they both thought he was going to heave the piece of wood he was carrying across the room, but somehow he maintained control.

'Get out of the way, Bill. Come on, bugger off out of it.'

Dwyer took over tending the grate, then gave up, and turned to the fireplace instead. Starting afresh with more room to work in, he soon had a weak fire going and the damp wood hissed in the heat. It was going, but only just. Dwyer knew it would take hours before there was any warmth in the room, and knowing also that dinner would be very late. Tonight the stew would be cooked on the embers in the fireplace and the stove was left for tomorrow.

Both kids made themselves scarce, and went about feeding the chooks and locking them away for the night. They were always careful with their poultry, what with free-ranging cats and dogs roaming their valley. The meal was the best that could be mustered given the circumstances, and silently consumed. There was a tension in the room, and it was still obvious later when Kitty cleared and washed the dishes. She did so as quietly as possible for fear of angering him further. They prepared for bed in their respective rooms, and in due course returned to bid him goodnight as had become the custom. He was still sitting in his armchair brooding, a half-empty bottle of beer sitting on the floor beside him. His sullen face staring aimlessly at burning soot twinkling in the back of the fireplace. He looked up when they entered the room and regarded them both with a sneer. Little had been said about their behaviour beyond that original outburst of his, but the kids could see it was still on his mind.

'Come here... you too, Kitty,' he said with what seemed to be an unnecessary sternness in his voice. 'As far as I'm concerned it's high time you accepted that I'm in charge here. You are both well overdue for a good hiding, and tonight that's exactly what you're going to get.'

In the past there had been only a few instances when the Wilsons had had to raise their voices at them. Rarely had they received even a mild cuff around the ears, and that had usually been sufficient if either had been playing up a bit. Both Bill and Kitty had been brought up, however, to obey instructions from adults, and did so without question. Uncle Jim, now standing and silhouetted against the fire seemed huge and menacing. He ranted on for some minutes about respect and responsibilities. His lecture was clear and to the point. He would tolerate no argument. For their part, they felt it best not to say anything anyway, unless a response was called for.

'Do you understand then?' he said, in a quieter less harsh voice.

'Yes Uncle Jim,' they chorused in little more than a whisper, hoping that was the end of it.

'Right then, we'll have you first.'

Kitty listened to his instructions with lower lip quivering. From the tone of his voice it would have been folly to defy him. Without hesitation she gathered her nightie up around her waist, and bent over the end of the couch. In the past they had been a rather reserved family. With rooms of their own they had always enjoyed privacy and freedom from observation. On this occasion modesty took second place to obedience. There was a long pause, as he seemed to consider his options. Then, without further delay, he withdrew his belt and folded it into a short thick strap.

• • • • • • •

Dwyer stepped outside and lit a cigarette. He could hear both kids crying in their rooms. Their sobs seemed exaggerated to him, but thankfully the sound was almost drowned out by water pouring noisily from rotted guttering. The deluge from clouds pregnant with rain had been a constant background noise for some time now. He looked at the dark sky and muttered aloud. 'We could have done with this back home.' And then in a louder voice, 'Shut up in there, you two.'

'Wretched kids,' he thought to himself. Scrawny little runts. Jim found his seat on the veranda in the semi-darkness, and moved it further back from the wet. He sat, and thought back to his Australian outback days. They were good times. Hard but good. The weather had been against the two of them most of the time though. He and his wife had done their best on a difficult piece of land. But he thought now of how those last rainstorms, those gully-washers that dumped on them once in a blue moon, had followed one after the other. A whole series of them. There had been nothing they could do but watch. Swollen streams where nothing had run before had raged unchecked. The subsequent flooding over what seemed like hundreds of miles had devastated their property. And when the water receded, the sun turned a muddy aftermath into a crust like concrete and then to dust. He thought of the view from his shaded wide veranda back home when things had been better. Gentle flat to rolling country in the immediate foreground, but thereafter a beige hue for miles. Virtually nothing for as far as the eye could see. Plenty of dust though and plenty of heat. Only one stock unit to ten acres compared to the three ewes to an acre around here. Yes the outback had been harsh on the animals, and also on its people. He had been lucky to sell, and to get a fairly good price too. Yes, he had been lucky. But even so, he regretted having ever come over here.

'Should have stayed where I was,' he muttered to himself again through clenched teeth. But he knew that with his wife's death, there would have been many changes to adapt to in any event.

Damn kids. Boisterous, loud, undisciplined. Just bloody liabilities. Should knock their bloody heads together and bury them in the compost heap. The worms would finish the job. It was a thought he dwelled on for a while as he contemplated a quieter life without ties.

In those first weeks he had put up with a lot, having made allowance for their parent's deaths. They seemed to have got over the whole situation rather quickly, however, and now their exuberance irked him. Both kids had had fair warning, but those threats had gone unheeded. It seemed that way to him anyway. And it had not worried him that he had finally resorted to the belt. It was unlikely to be the last time either. Clearly neither had been punished properly before. Spoilt brats. Where he had come from, a good leathering from time to time did no one any harm. And it brought with it a deal of respect that was not evident over here. He found it easy to justify his actions this evening, and would demand a marked change from these two. He needed to be able to rely more on Bill's help. Needed to curb Kitty's lip too. She was a little too smart for her own good, and if need be they could expect more of the same. Eventually he flicked a half-smoked cigarette out into the dark and went inside, slamming the door on the rain. It was good to return to the warmth, even though the fire was still struggling. With wetted finger and thumb he carefully retrieved a couple of embers that lay glowing on the hearth, then stretched his legs out with damp socks steaming in front of him. Settled back on the couch, he was soon asleep and snoring loudly. Dwyer spent the whole night there.

Soft shafts of morning light filtered in through the curtains and disturbed the kids' sleep. An overall quietness indicated the poor weather had moved on. Morning brought with it memories of the previous night's events, and both of them were taking extra care not to upset Uncle Jim. By the time Bill was up and dressed, Kitty was already setting the kitchen table. Their uncle had risen earliest, lit the stove, and was quietly going about his business with the frying pan. It was strange not to hear the usual morning's chatter. Few words were spoken over breakfast, and once finished he gathered his work things together and was off. Before he left, however, Dwyer reeled off a list of things he wanted them to do. He paid no regard to the fact they had school to attend as well.

'And you can finish off putting the chopped stuff under the lean-to, Bill. I've put logs that can wait till next year on the roof where they can weather a season or two. Just mind you don't knock the supports too much.'

He strode off, grinning to himself as he passed by the structure with its precarious load balanced on the iron roofing.

They ran hard to catch up with school friends this morning, for it had been a late start.

'How's your bum?' Bill said, trying a weak smile when they eventually slowed to a jog.

'Don't be so personal,' Kitty responded curtly, not wanting to discuss the matter.

'Did it hurt?'

'Of course. And he probably whacked me harder because I'm the oldest. We'll just have to be careful not to anger him again. Now shut up, I don't want to talk about it. And don't you say anything to the others either.'

Both kids seemed to forget any difficulties at home once they got inside the gates. It was an interesting school, and apparently dated back at least a hundred years. The buildings were old, but not the original ones they had been told. Nevertheless, Bill often thought of all those students who had gone before him, particularly those whose names appeared on the 'Shields of Honour' strategically placed around the hall where their daily assembly was held. There were no unhappy students here and, with a small roll, they all seemed to do pretty well at their studies. He knew he was not the best student in his class at any particular subject, but he did enjoy school. Bill's teacher had noticed other qualities in him, and placed the youngster in charge of certain classroom duties. His friends did not mind taking orders from Bill, and he easily assumed this privileged position.

During interval and lunch breaks there was an almost deafening noise in the quadrangle as everyone chased, laughed and shouted. The girls were always squealing. And the boys all reckoned it was because they had fleas and teased them mercilessly. Nevertheless they were all very good friends, and when it was fine the walk home was always fun. There were about five kids living up their road. They would pick on each other and run ahead and hide, and made use of numerous spots to jump out and frighten each other.

A deep pool below one of the bridges always delayed them for at least ten minutes. Today the water drifted past lazily, but there had been times when it had been a frighteningly rapid torrent. Hardly any rain was needed in the hills to change a tranquil scene like the one today into a dangerous flood. Leaning over the rail and dropping spitballs on leaves floating by was great sport. Bill was a pretty accurate 'bomber'. None of them had watches. That was a luxury kids simply did not have in those days. However, they all had chores of some description at home, and thankfully a fairly accurate inbuilt sense of time. Before long each of them made for his or her respective destination, Bill and Kitty included. And perhaps leaving a little earlier these days than they had done in the past.

Their desire to please Uncle Jim was brought about more by fear than out of consideration for him. He remained unpredictable, and their efforts often proved fruitless as he easily found fault. His mood at the time usually dictated the outcome, and as the months dragged by Bill and Kitty came to expect at least a couple of beltings each week. Dwyer had a perverted habit of watching them from the derelict shed. He would slip in there for a smoke, squint through the cracks, and accuse them later of the many things he had observed.

They came to believe they were forever under his gaze. Because Bill and Kitty always avoided the Weta Shed, it never dawned on them that anyone would actually go in there. It was his little sanctuary from where he could carry out his spying.

Thankfully both toilet and bathroom remained a place where they could rely on some privacy. While dishing out his punishment, however, he always delighted in making it as humiliating as possible. When dealing with Kitty, he liked to have Bill up close watching the action and vice versa. Once bent over the arm of that couch, neither dared move in case it infuriated him further. Often he did not hit hard, but he rarely gave less than eight whacks. He insisted they count the number out loud, and always made it a drawn out affair. It was horrible treatment, frequently unnecessary, and they loathed him for it.

'So much for promising to look after us,' Kitty whispered to her brother once out of their uncle's hearing on one occasion.

Dwyer rarely visited the local hotel these days. Not for any particular reason. And even though he enjoyed the company there, he gave it a miss most week nights. In many ways he was still a loner, not wanting to establish an expectation from others that he was one of the regulars. If he ever had to quietly move on, this way it was unlikely he would be missed. There were only two pubs now with their respective hard-core groups of drinkers. The one he had favoured had been built back in the late 1800s, and was originally one of many such establishments that had lined the main street. It stood alone at the end of the township, having always been the most popular watering hole and having stood the test of time as a result. For current patrons, as had been the case with their fathers and their fathers before them, it was where evenings were spent. Those few times when Dwyer strayed from the quiet of his home and joined the regulars he would come home well and truly 'tanked up'. The country's six o'clock closing rule was not strictly observed in these parts, so he often arrived on the doorstep well after 8.00 p.m. Bill and Kitty were lucky when he just wanted to go to bed. If not, his general belligerence increased the likelihood of some nit-picking argument, and he would latch onto a minor issue with the usual repercussions. He hated being their guardian, and appeared to look for reasons to blame them, as if it was their fault he had been left in this role. Either that, or he gained a perverted enjoyment from displaying the power he had over them both. Whatever the reason, their recent loss of loved ones was not something that in any way curbed his anger towards them. In fact, with time it seemed almost to intensify.

In next to no time the children were experiencing yet another heart wrenching incident, thankfully on this occasion only a near-tragedy. It happened on the way back from school. Just the two of them today, walking home slowly, still wondering how their future would unfold with Mum and Dad no longer there each day. Some months had passed now, but still there were bad patches when all they could think of was the car accident and how horrible it would have been for their parents. How horrible it was for them these days too, living with Uncle Jim.

Bill was a few yards ahead when they reached the bridge, and he paused, leaning over the rail as he always did, and dropped a few frothy 'spit bombs'. On the edge of the creek lay a sack, wet and heavy-looking, which had managed to float to the edge of the bank before becoming caught up on a snag.

'Probably a townie dumping rubbish,' he thought, until something convinced him to look closer. From that distance he was not sure, but it seemed to be moving. He stared long and hard, convinced it had moved by itself.

'Hey, Kitty, come and have a look at this,' he shouted loudly.

Bill was already clambering quickly down the bank, and Kitty rushed to the side rail, not understanding what had caused his excitement. He slid down the clay slope, heaved himself over logs that had built up in the last flood, and splashed through knee-deep water with no regard at all for clothing or school shoes. She could see her brother was on a mission. Even so, Bill was sensible enough to ensure the long razor-edged leaves did not slit him when pushing his way through patches of head-high cutty-grass. Emerging unscathed from the rough foliage, he grabbed the sack before it slipped from its insecure position into deeper water. And then holding up high for Kitty to see, the skinny, waterlogged and shivering body of a puppy.

'It's alive,' he yelled triumphantly.

Dwyer looked at the creature with scorn written all over his face. It was too young for him to tell its parentage, so he had no idea whether it might eventually develop into a decent enough hunting dog he could use. His first thoughts were that it had been the runt of a litter, and so why would anyone want it. No wonder it had been dumped. But then the scowl on his face softened, and the young boy who waited eagerly for a response to his request saw some faint approval growing in the man's expression.

'Not so fast, Bill, we've got some matters to discuss first. For one thing, feeding it and cleaning up is your responsibility. Remember you've got other chores around here and you're often behind with those.'

'Yes Uncle Jim, there won't be any problem with that. Oh please,' Bill pleaded.

'We'll both get up at stupid o'clock if necessary to get our work done,' Kitty contributed with a laugh.

'And another thing, I don't want to be stepping in any dog crap around here, so the mutt can stay down the back. You'll not be having it sleeping inside or any nonsense like that.'

Bill agreed to anything and everything. He held the warm fluffy body up under his chin, and received a face-full of licks for his trouble. It was going to be the start of a long friendship. Kitty loved the pup too, but right from the start it was Bill's dog and he named her Trixie. Trix for short. Uncle Jim helped make a box to stuff under the shed, and although too small for the chain that was still attached to one of the supporting piles, he said it would not be too long before she was big enough to want to sleep out under the stars. Dwyer seemed to share Bill and Kitty's affection for the dog, and it helped take attention away from recent incidents. Perhaps things had started to improve.

The doctor visited their place after an accident at the mill. He had no name, or so it seemed. Just known politely as the doctor, or in Jim Dwyer's book as 'Doc'.

He arrived in his big old Ford. Bill said afterwards he had seen the car before. In town it had always looked black and shiny. He probably regretted having to bring it out here on the back roads. Today it was almost completely grey with dust.

'You've been lifting stuff incorrectly, Jim. It's a bad muscle strain but I've got the remedy if you can get it rubbed into the right area. You'll need bed rest for as long as possible. Get someone to use this on you,' they heard him being told.

'It'll be time off work then, Doc?'

'Bed's the best place, otherwise it's going to be an ongoing problem. At least a week off, maybe two.'

Jim complained but would do as he was told. He had sense enough to know it was the only remedy, despite an obvious loss of pay.

'Kitty and Bill will take turn about staying at home with me. They're good helpers, Doc.'

Sure to his word, he kept them on the run, remaking the bed, bringing more wood for the fire, a fresh pot of tea or another session of back rubbing to ease his discomfort.

Earlier it had looked as if the relationship between them all had taken a good step forward. The injury changed that, however, and Dwyer reverted to his old self.

'Get that bloody horse liniment again will you!' he would often yell.

It became a regular demand, with Kitty attending to him mostly, and sometimes again well after Bill had gone to bed. He appeared to gain the best relief when it was applied later in the evening, enabling him to sleep throughout the night. Kitty appeared to be more effective at applying it than Bill, who would be almost asleep in his room when she was called. His bedroom was off the main living area. The other two were next to each other at the front of the house. There would be a faint tapping on the wall, and he would hear her collecting the liniment and the sound of bare feet on floorboards. He could never make out the muffled words coming from Uncle Jim's room. When she returned the house would at last become quiet.

Kitty changed. She became sullen, fell behind with some of her schoolwork, and often ignored her brother, with no time for Trix either. Bill knew she was tired. They both were. His sister appeared to just accept the routine. It was part of her makeup anyway, whereas Bill was full of adventure and high-jinks so long as it harmed no one. He smothered Trix with constant attention, but still found time to help Kitty with her share of the chores as best he could. They both longed for the day when Uncle Jim could return to work fit and well. It happened a fortnight later when the bottle of medication finally ran out. At last there was no further need for his treatment, and they could all look forward to a proper night's sleep again.

CHAPTER 8

Dwyer had become used to lying around the place, so a return to work was something that did not hold much appeal. During his time at home he had thought of hunting trips he might fit in when feeling better, before an inevitable need to generate some more income became necessary once again. He was unable to put those plans into action, however, and the daily ritual of leaving for the mill recommenced.

Returning home one day, and obviously in a foul mood, they heard him stamping up the steps muttering, cursing and kicking off his boots.

'Bill, come and clean this. That bloody dog of yours...'

The angry words trailed off into nothing, but it was clear he had missed a bit earlier on when cleaning up and of course Uncle Jim had stepped in it. Bill grabbed the boot and a small stick to clean out the cleats. What a stink. He made sure no water got inside the footwear later when washing the last of it off. That would have been the last straw. Dwyer fumed but said nothing. It had been one of those days already, and he sat by the fire muttering to himself and drinking.

'Bloody dog will have to go,' he said with raised voice before staring into the fire again. Bill said nothing. It was best not to.

Uncle Jim thumped around the house for ages after they had gone to bed, and finally found what he had been looking for in the storage locker. His machete. He sat back by the fire testing its weight, feeling the keenness of the blade, giving it a few swings through the air as his smelly damp socks steamed away in front of him. The warmth of the fire was always comforting after a stressful day and helped calm his natural irritability. After an hour or two, it was good to get outside for a last breath of fresh night air before turning in.

When the house rose the next morning, it was the usual rush to get things organised before he left for work and the kids got away to school. There was no evidence of Bill's furry friend, which was unusual because although free to wander these days, she was always there at meal times.

'Trix, Trix, Trix!' he called up and down the driveway, fearing she may have wandered out to the road. There was still no sign when it was time to go, and despite Kitty's assistance they eventually had to leave the matter until after school.

Kitty was doing her best to reassure him. 'Trixy will be waiting when we get home. You can count on that. She's probably gone exploring up the paddock.'

Dwyer seemed not the least bit concerned, simply listing the few things he wanted done by the time he returned. Then he was gone.

They never saw Trix again. Dwyer said she was probably carried off by one of the hawks flying around here. Bill had his doubts, and called her morning and night, up and down the road. Eventually Dwyer told him to get over it and to stop acting like a baby. A week or so later, Bill found the blood-splattered machete in the storage room, and his worst fears were confirmed at the sight of the matted fluff on its blade. In the quiet of the bedroom he cried at the thought of what had been done, but decided he would not give his uncle the satisfaction of knowing he was aware of the man's cruelty. But in his heart Bill knew he could never trust Uncle Jim again, and he doubted the intense hatred he felt would ever lessen. He could stand the beltings, but this was different. There would be a day of reckoning, he decided, but at his age he could not really visualise it happening.

One night after many weeks of so-called harmony the strained peace was again broken. Bill often thought of the sequence of events. It was their last night in that house. The night they finally made a break from Jim Dwyer's demands and constant bullying. Kitty was once again in the firing line, and the latest accusation centred on a handful of crumbs under the kitchen table, of all things. She had gathered up the cloth incorrectly, and he was quick to latch on to what he referred to as 'her casual approach to duties'. Such a petty misdemeanour, but then again he had been drinking. What else could they expect?

'You lazy little bitch,' he slurred.

'I didn't do it,' she shouted back, defiantly.

Kitty was annoyed that after all her hard work lately, she was being blamed for something any one of them could have done accidentally, Uncle Jim included.

'Don't you raise your voice at me, madam,' he spat back pointing his finger menacingly.

As always, it was not advisable to intervene. Any further protesting from her, or interference on Bill's part, increased the risk and severity of punishment. He was thankful when she elected not to continue her argument. But Jim kept on at her, goading and testing her patience. On rare occasions, acceptance of wrongdoing and an apology was sometimes enough to settle the matter. Kitty said nothing more this time. Clearly her silence was frustrating him, and he finished with the usual menacing words through clenched teeth and with his narrow-eyed look.

'You're for it later. You're really for it this time.'

When Dwyer had made a decision, it was irreversible. Both kids knew nothing more would be said or done until after their meal. They hoped, as always, that he might forget. It was a long shot, but after-dinner drowsiness in front of the fire sometimes had that effect on him. Once the sun dropped behind the ridge, the valley quickly cooled in the late afternoon shade.

'There's a real nip in the air,' Bill whispered to Kitty when he re-entered the room with an armful of wood. 'It'll be dark soon. Probably only one or two stars tonight.'

The couch was on castors, and they positioned it closer to the fire and quietly attended to school work for a while. It was good having an older sister who could provide much-needed help with arithmetic. He found it so much easier having it explained away from the classroom hustle and bustle and other distractions. Kitty had always been prepared to help, and they finished both lots of homework before settling back with a pile of out-of-date magazines. Uncle Jim was not at all interested in their progress at school and never made any enquiries.

'Look at him, only half-way through his bottle of beer and already asleep.'

Dwyer had begun to snore. He was slumped awkwardly in his chair and did not seem at all comfortable. Not an attractive sight. Unshaven and with dribble coming from the corner of his open mouth.

'Perhaps he'll sleep the whole night there. Let's pack these things away and get off to bed. I bags the bathroom first,' whispered Kitty. She ran a bath, but Bill decided to wait until morning for his wash.

As usual the bedroom smelt damp and clammy. It was the same elsewhere in the house other than in their living room. There were tiny gaps in most walls. Even some you could put your fingers through, and although there were spy holes in his room where you could just see the flames, no warmth ventured far from the fireplace. Tonight it seemed as windy inside as out and bitterly cold. Bill snuggled under his blankets to avoid the draughts and sleep quickly took over.

It seemed only minutes later that a distant noise disturbed him. In his befuddled state he lay for a while getting his bearings, eventually realising it was his Uncle Jim's voice in the next room that had woken him. Slipping quietly to the floor, he paused briefly on all fours, then crept forward to investigate.

'Get in here right now Kitty, you insolent little brat.'

In the dark of his room Bill remained motionless, straining to hear the discussion. 'Here we go again,' he thought, listening as Dwyer ranted on about her poor housekeeping efforts. He was in a right mood.

'Get out here at once.'

The man was not going to let the matter rest and raised his voice even louder, demanding her immediate presence with the threat he would come in and drag her out if need be. There was silence for a moment, and Bill eased his eye up towards the thin beam of light shining through one of the cracks. He assumed Uncle Jim had been woken by the sound of her bath water. It had a tendency to make loud gurgling sounds as it drained away. A sort of gulping noise in the pipes.

'I'll come in,' he said again, 'unless you get out here right now.'

Bill heard the familiar sound of the bathroom door squeaking open, and he repositioned himself slightly. Without any chance to dry herself, or to get dressed, it was a very timid-looking Kitty who entered the room with only a towel and an armful of clothing pressed against her as protection. She cautiously edged her way around the room, keeping her back to the wall. Bill could see them both now. His tall shape silhouetted against the fire, hers off to one side lit by flickering flames that danced about, casting weird shadows and bright splashes of light on the walls. Kitty stood with dripping wet hair, and shook as he continued to yell. And then with two purposeful steps he crossed the gap, his powerful fingers closing on one arm above her elbow. Lifting the youngster on to tip toes, he marched her back to the fire light, sneering at the expression frozen on her face as she scrabbled along beside him. He paraded her back and forth about the room, pointing out the mess.

Bill watched as Uncle Jim released her and began removing his belt. Kitty, in turn, struggled to do something about her state of undress but it was a fruitless attempt. Wet body, tangle of clothing, and all the time trying to keep that towel in place. Uncle Jim was too quick, too strong, and had no trouble yet again manhandling her towards the fireplace. Kitty lost everything she had when he kicked furniture into position, swung the unresisting body up high and draped her over the back of the couch. It only took one hand to grasp both arms firmly behind her back. She was helpless, naked, and now with Uncle Jim's frame in the way, somewhere beyond Bill's view. The thrashing began in earnest. Slumped back against the cold bedroom wall, he began counting to himself. Her initial refusal to cry made Dwyer all the more determined, and he brought the strap down hard, again and again and again. She eventually gave in, but he did not stop. Bill counted eight before she made a sound. And then another ten.

Crawling back between the sheets, and doing his best not to make the bed creak, he placed his hands over his ears, partially to keep them warm and partially to block out any further noise. Tonight, sleep was unlikely to come easily, and during the next hour or so an urgent plan began to unfold in his mind.

Dwyer left her where she was, regarding her with utter contempt as he re-threaded his belt. Curled up in a small ball on the floor her sobbing gradually became a whimper as she lay, refusing to make eye contact with him. He retired to his own room and hunted out his packet of fags.

'Shut up, Kitty, just shut that bloody racket up,' he shouted back through the wall, not at all concerned he might disturb her brother. The noise was immediately stifled for fear of further consequences. Yes, he had dealt to her severely tonight, Jim thought as he undressed himself. Probably gone a bit too far. But she deserved every bit of it, he smugly reassured himself. Had not planned it, the way it turned out — her clothes off and all that. Just happened that way. Thankfully the boy was asleep.

He sat on his bed thinking of her and smirked. Just recently, when he had been poorly, Kitty had treated his injured back with rubbing cream. She had been a considerate nurse. It was always cold in the bedrooms. One night after attending to him, he had coaxed her into his bed to warm her up. He was aware her own room had become damp. Bill's usually was too. Her sheets would have been cold while his bed-clothing had been warm. He had wondered whether that was the attraction that chilly evening. Perhaps she was just uncertain of his reaction had she indicated a preference not to. She was, after all, rather a nervous kid at the best of times. There seemed to have been no hesitation though, and she had slipped beneath the covers and faced away from him. It was cosy, and Kitty seemed to drop off to sleep quickly. She was just a kid. Later on his roaming hands had told him otherwise. He doubted she would have known. But if aware of his fondling, she had kept it to herself. He assumed she had not mentioned it to the boy. He decided she was unlikely to have said anything, and he was pleased for that. When he had first arrived in New Zealand, she was definitely a child. But she had changed in recent months. Maybe she liked it, he kidded himself. It had become an established routine over the following few weeks. But each night he eventually had to wake her and send her back to her own room.

Tonight he retired to his bedroom alone. He usually smoked outside, but this time he made an exception. With the light out, only the glow from his cigarette lit the walls as he drew in each lungful. He was unable to take his mind off Kitty, and wondered how far he could actually go with her. Some hours later there was a soft bump outside. Then another. He raised himself on his elbows and listened for a while. Nothing. Lying back, he dismissed it as something the wind had blown over. Probably those boards stacked against the washhouse. There was a stillness that made him uneasy, however, and a silence within the house that seemed out of place this time. It was difficult to get to sleep but eventually he did. And he slept soundly.

• • • • • • •

Helping Kitty safely out the window had been a nerve-wracking experience. Getting the window open in the first place even more difficult. And every moment there was the risk Uncle Jim would burst in on them.

'The paint has stuck it in its frame.'

'Well try harder, but do it quietly,' she urged.

He worked away for a good ten minutes, but in the end Bill gave up trying to ease it open gently. With a final heave the sash window slid up, letting in a blast of cold night air.

Kitty had tiptoed into his room earlier, and they had agreed there and then they had both had enough. It was very much a spur of the moment decision, although individually they had thought about running away many times before.

'We haven't prepared for this properly,' Bill whispered.

Kitty had shoes in one hand, and her longs and a jersey screwed up in the other.

'You'll have to get some warm clothes, Bill, and we'll take a blanket each from your bed.'

Thankfully his bedroom window was furthermost from Uncle Jim's end of the house.

At the very last moment Kitty hesitated and turned to Bill.

'I don't know,' she stammered, 'it might make everything worse.'

'He killed Trix, Kitty. I'm sorry. I wasn't going to tell you.'

If there had been any doubt in her mind before, it was now gone. With the minimum of possessions, they left what warmth and security the house held and fled across the paddock. He turned once and looked back at the home he had loved so much since the day he had first arrived, and looked instead at a shapeless building he now loathed for the memories it held. There was no sign of Uncle Jim. It was as Bill imagined escaping from jail might have been like as they bent low and ran. A biting wind tugged at their bodies, and while they realised the bush would be just as cold, at least it would afford some protection from the elements. It was cloudy too and that was a God-send.

'We're lucky there's no moon. Usually these paddocks are bathed in moonlight.'

Although the surroundings were familiar, it was so very different at night and took longer than they envisaged getting out of sight of the house. At any moment the kids expected to sense the thump of Jim's footsteps behind them, and hear the frightening bellow of his voice.

'Following the boundary fence will be the most direct route.'

It was a struggle making their way uphill, even with the fence as a guideline. Weighty cumbersome blankets did not help at this stage either, and with both arms full they found it almost impossible at times. The hay barn was soon reached. Half-way up the slope, but out of sight of the house, it became their first resting spot and a chance to recover and gather thoughts. Hay had always looked attractive as a bed, but in fact was dusty and full of prickles. Despite the protection this shelter gave them, they soon felt the need to press on. Once inside the bush they believed the going would be easier. It was not. Bill had forgotten how dark it could be in there. Animal tracks, particularly through the ferned gullies, left large areas without vegetation and it was in one of these spots that they lay down and spent the rest of their first night in the open.

'Thank God for the blankets.'

On the high ground above them it began to snow lightly. Kitty felt the change in temperature and huddled closer, taking advantage of her brother's body heat. Many thoughts went through her mind, but despite the discomfort there was definitely no going back. Bill would look after her.

'Time to go,' he murmured at last, 'it must be about five o'clock and he'll be waking soon.'

Neither had a watch of course. It was just a guess.

The cold made him grateful he had brought his emergency kit, a small package he had made up months ago. Something he had thought of that might come in handy one day in the form of a candle, wax matches, some dry paper, all wrapped up in greaseproof paper. Even one of Uncle Jim's razor blades, retrieved from the rubbish bin, and a bit of string. Just a simple survival pack. It would enable him to make a fire if they had to stay out another night.

'You know, it's Sunday and he'll have all day to track us down. And he'll probably bring Holloway and his dogs.'

'Yeah, and once they've tracked us to the barn they'll have a fair idea of our direction.'

Bill knew the bush well, having been up here many times before with Able. It was one of their hideaway areas. But today he and Kitty would venture deeper into the bush than he had ever been before, with no clue where they would come out or what their plan might be from then on. They headed upwards with caution, gaining ground in the hope of eventually getting their bearings. Bill tried as best he could to keep in a straight line. The last thing they wanted was to risk going in a circle. And it was possible to do this. Once before he had lost direction on a bit of a plateau when heading up hill, and ended up back at the start when all the time thinking he was descending the other side of the ridge. They were fighting against time, and occasionally fighting against patches of supplejack too. The duo made little headway. Finger-thick supplejack vines formed a tangled barrier as far ahead as they could see. There was nothing to do but to continue to force a passage through. It took precious minutes to cover even the shortest of distances, and the delay was worrying Bill. Without a set destination, his only wish was to put as many miles as possible between them and Uncle Jim.

Bill had learned a lot about the bush from his Dad, and also later from Uncle Jim. He felt he now knew a fair bit about hunting and the bush. But Jim was a stalker with many years' experience. And they were going to be up against that. Up against someone who had been described by more than one person as being 'as cunning as a Maori dog'.

Dwyer woke with a start. Morning already, but surprisingly without those usual sounds of Kitty doing her thing in the kitchen.

'Is that jug on yet?' he called out, in a tone that demanded some activity in the house.

He raised himself on his elbows and pulled the curtain to one side. Frost-covered paddocks greeted him. 'Almost a Christmas card scene,' he thought.

'There's no doubting the beauty of the countryside on a clear winter's day,' he called out, keen to have the fire going and rashers of bacon spitting in the pan.

'Hope you've got plenty of dry wood ready, Bill. Come on you two, get those feet on the floor.'

He was in good spirits despite the previous night's incident, and despite the morning's cold which could so easily have kept everyone under the covers.

'Things to do today,' he shouted, but louder this time as he quickly finished dressing.

Both bedroom doors remained shut and the silence spoke heaps. It was obvious they were not still in bed. He knew something was up even before he entered their rooms. The missing clothing and blankets told it all. Out on the veranda he shaded his eyes against the rising sun and scanned the paddocks. He was annoyed they were off playing somewhere, and shouted their names several times. But then he just stood there and quietly fumed, thinking the worst. There were tracks in the grass but they were not clear enough. 'Must have left before the frost,' he muttered. Nevertheless, he suspected they would not have gone far, and guessed if they had done a runner would soon be regretting their decision.

Dwyer prepared breakfast for himself and used up all the bacon. They could go without. He assumed they would return and he smiled to himself. Out on the veranda, with frying pan in hand, he stood and let the aroma waft forth. He thought the smell would bring them out of hiding if not too far away. They would be sorry. Oh yes he would make them sorry all right. Later, he found where they had gone through the window and the significance of the noises in the night dawned on him. He smirked. The pieces began to come together.

'So they have had a pretty good start,' he mused as he put one or two items together in his knapsack. The day was well underway when he found where he assumed the kids had spent the night in the hay barn. It was sited in a shaded and protected place and the surrounding ground had retained its frosty white mantle. Their route from there was quite clear until the tracks disappeared on warmer ground. They were heading for the bush and would probably make for the tops where the going would be easier. He needed to catch them well before then he decided, and headed off at a run. Inconvenient though it was for him, he smirked again at the thought of the hunt ahead of him. He would enjoy running them down like the frightened animals they were. It was not long before the smile left his face, however, as Dwyer found himself blocked by the same tangle of vegetation the kids had faced earlier.

'Bloody bush lawyer,' he muttered out loud as the barbed vine grabbed at his balaclava.

'Curse this bush and curse those kids.'

He paused. Listening. Waiting for a tell-tale noise. Nothing. Nothing but the normal sounds he expected to hear. The animal tracks meandered back and forth. They seemed to have no purpose, no direction, and eventually led to what appeared to him to be an illogical destination. He decided it was easier to make his own way and had a fair idea which way that was. More or less straight up. He skirted the mix of smooth supplejack and barbed vines altogether. It took a while to find a way around, but overall it was faster and easier than fighting his way through it. He knew that much from experience. The going was better once he was able to follow a ridgeline where undergrowth was sparsely scattered amongst the trees. He could jog along at a fair pace, so long as he continued to dance over the tangle of roots ahead. Trip on those, and he risked breaking a leg. Again, from experience, he knew the hardest part might well be just before reaching the snow line. He was right. Getting past the last battlefield of leatherwood was going to be a time-consuming exercise. Worse than supplejack it required patience, and that was something he usually practised when hunting, but a quality that was perhaps not so evident in him on other occasions.

Dwyer stopped often when in the bush. Stopped and listened. An act easily dismissed as laziness on his part, but anyone forming that opinion would have been wrong. When hunting, it was his patience that gave him an edge. It was early afternoon and beginning to drizzle again. He could do with a brew. He thought it was time for a fire and got his bits and pieces ready near a trickle of a stream. He only needed to boil a half cup. Twenty minutes, and he would be away again. Few would be as successful as he in lighting a fire in these conditions. He used a technique learned many years ago, but which meant getting wet as a result. Virtually everything burnable was damp. Nevertheless a fire could always be made, given time and a stub of candle. And he had both. The delay would be worth it. A chance to get his breath back, to gather his thoughts, to get something warm in him. It would give him renewed energy. A steady hand was needed to build his fire around the constant flame of a candle. He removed his oilskin, knowing that rainwater collecting in its folds would eventually run in rivulets as he crouched over the fire, quickly extinguishing his efforts. His wool jacket would get wet, but would remain warm enough despite this. It was slow work feeding slivers of drier wood sliced from a branch he had pulled down from above him. It was the only place worth looking for firewood. He had a sharp knife and that helped. Dwyer thought of how he had told Bill to always get dead wood off a tree, and not to try burning anything that had fallen to the forest floor where it quickly soaked up moisture from the ground.

'Ungrateful little brat,' he said out loud as if for the benefit of anyone within earshot.

His fire grew from a mass of match-like twigs to slightly bigger pieces, and so on. At the start they flared and lasted only seconds. But each one helped the next, and with plenty of new wood at hand he soon had a small fire going with enough heat to dry some of the larger bits. He fed it and kept the momentum going until satisfied the flames would last. It was almost twenty minutes before he felt confident enough to introduce his utensil containing just a splash of water to the embers. It was time Dwyer felt worth spending as he counted on being out all day and probably overnight too. He was pleased he had had the foresight to bring a bit of gear.

It took only a short while to heat the small quantity of water, and at last he had his drink. Even with small sips the coffee scalded his tongue. That, together with the discomfort of drinking from a tin cup straight from the coals. It was good though. He felt a measure of comfort from simply squatting there and clasping the hot mug close to his face. The drips from foliage above him finished off the dying embers, and he smudged the remains into the dirt with a boot. He had to move on. Time was now of the essence with the day half-gone. It was easy to delay longer while surrounding bush afforded some protection from the wind. But he gathered his gear and studied the dirty weather as best he could from the stream bed before heading upward again. It would take a good half-hour to get to the bushline. There was no defined track, and he had a leatherwood barrier to contend with yet.

The 'army of soldiers' stood in front of him, with each bush petrified and stunted. Struggling with springy and obstinate branches, he found those that broke, snapped into even sharper points. Had it been witnessed, his patience would have been applauded. But his lack of agility let him down, and with both skills being tested again and again, frustration finally took over as he lost balance in the shrubbery yet again when it refused to give way. Some considerable time later he emerged with shirt torn and arms scratched. There was a look of annoyance about him, but he was nevertheless triumphant. At last, with only tussock covering the terrain ahead, he could make up lost time. Dwyer crouched there momentarily in the snowgrass. It was an opportunity to settle his heaving chest and also to regain his bearings. The mist swirled around him, and then just as suddenly cleared. The silence was unnerving. He had left his oilskin off. Stalking experience over the years had shown him he could move more quietly without it. He had a general idea he was heading in the right direction but was hesitant to commit himself so soon. In the past he had tramped for hours, and then retraced his steps because of poor judgement. It had usually been brought on by tiredness. Today he knew he was tired, and needed to make allowance for it.

A few slips and natural hollows sheltered away from the sun's reach still contained patches of snow, and it crunched underfoot. Apart from that, the only real sign of winter was the wind, which served to clear the mist from time to time. A rocky outcrop ahead on the highest piece of ground would afford a view in all directions. He stopped half-way up, not wanting to silhouette himself against the skyline. Another hunting trick of his and another chance to recover. A cigarette was needed, and he used the time to search the ridge ahead of him. Usually these tops were covered in cloud, and this was the first time he had actually been up here. He had always kept well down in the bush on past shooting excursions. It was probably still raining down there. 'Quite a view all right,' he thought to himself. It was a strange feeling, climbing above the weather, and looking down on a sea of cloud. For a moment he wondered why he even bothered chasing these two. But he knew why he had to catch them this time. He could not afford to have them mouth off tales to all and sundry in the heat of the moment. Had to stop them at all costs.

CHAPTER 9

He drew once again on his fag and thought of his past in Australia. To those who had known him over the years, Jim and Tilly's marriage had been a happy one. Childless, but nevertheless happy. There was another side to this man though. Friends and family, particularly Tilly, had been unaware of Dwyer's unfaithfulness.

'Those girls,' he thought to himself. Casual workers. Usually kids just passing through looking for work. A brief stopover for some, while others had stayed on for a while. There was always a bit of employment to be found if prepared to accept lodgings and only a token wage. He had made three or four pregnant, and then encouraged them to move on. He preferred the European girls. Seen them off when he had had his fun though. Could hardly afford that type of embarrassment. Being a married man, the boss and all that. One had not cooperated. No one had asked after her the following day. That was the way with farm workers in transit. Here one day, gone the next. Only Dwyer knew the true contents of the rubbish heap. A pit of debris that was never going to be touched. Best place for the bitch, he had decided. The gollies, well they had no employment prospects at all in the towns, so took what was available in places such as his. If they misbehaved then they knew they would be punished, one way or another. In fact, he often looked for faults when Tilly was unable to perform her wifely duties, simply so he could get them into his shed. A bit on the side was part of normal life for him. He rarely went more than a week without that sort of activity.

Now he was lonely again. There was not a fatherly bone in him either. Probably best they had been childless. He accepted that, but did not see it as a failing in any way. This current role was not of his choosing but he had stayed. 'Heaven knows why,' he thought.

His mind turned to Kitty. He sneered as he remembered her small warm body. He continued to sneer as he thought of the situation that previous evening when she was squirming in his arms. Exposed and wet. His imagination took over. He was thinking she was old enough now for something a bit more serious. He would have some proper fun with her from now on. She was unlikely to talk if he kept her under control and continued to be free with the strap. He was confident enough of that. She had not complained to anyone so far.

His eyes narrowed. He focused on a spot well into the distance. A trick of light or was it movement? No, there it was again.

'I'm onto them,' he told himself aloud, as if needing to hear the confirmation.

'Little bastards.'

Further down the ridge two shapes left open ground and entered the protection of the cool bush. They paused briefly and looked back in Dwyer's direction, but with the sun low in the sky, and now in their eyes, they saw nothing untoward. Bill and Kitty moved forward slowly, unaware he was moving in on them. Dwyer waited until they were out of sight, then started towards the spot at a run. It was clear ahead of him, and a chance to close the distance. He thought this might be his only opportunity, and kept his eyes on the patch of vegetation where he had seen them last. Once inside that natural cover, he could easily lose them without the aid of dogs. His stalking skills came to the fore, and he gathered his thoughts as he slowed. They needed only to be sitting down and resting inside the bush line. He could so easily crash straight past them. It would be disastrous if he showed himself too early, or somehow got ahead of them. There were a few tarns between him and his quarry too. Some of these ridge-top ponds were iced over at the edges. They all looked deep and the ground around them soft. It was the peat that gave the impression of something dark and bottomless, and for this reason too he chose to slow down and avoid a mishap. In any event he did not want wet boots, and so gave the water as wide a berth as possible without losing sight of their entry point into the bush. It was a spot fixed in his mind as he covered the last of the ground. He thought he could hear voices ahead of him now, and it was clear they were taking a very casual approach to their escape from him.

• • • • • • •

'Let's rest again.'

'We should really keep going, but okay,' Bill said, trying to be as understanding as possible but at the same time mindful of the risk in delaying too long. He knew their Uncle Jim could catch up with them at any moment.

A suitable seat in the form of a fallen tree lay ahead of them. There must have been a storm through these parts some years ago, because up front they could see further evidence in the form of other uprooted trees. The one before them was the first in a series of decaying logs, and once up, it was obvious they could step from trunk to trunk and cover a good distance before returning to the ground. While resting Bill tried to reorganise their gear, for he was carrying their jerseys and raincoats, as well as the blankets, and it was all getting a bit too much. But with another sleep outside a very real likelihood, there was no point in jettisoning anything yet. It would be just as cold again tonight. With an arm around his sister's shoulders he pulled her close. He knew he had to protect her. Both were hungry, but neither had said anything to the other about it. Not so far, anyway. Today's tramp had left them feeling dirty and weak, and eventually Kitty spoke out.

'I'm dizzy.'

'It's probably because we haven't had breakfast or lunch,' he ventured, wishing they had planned this better and brought food with them. The prospect of having nothing to eat again as another meal-time passed by did not thrill him either. They sat quietly for a while.

'Uncle Jim touched me again the other night,' Kitty suddenly blurted out.

It was as if she had been trying to find the words or the right moment, but there it was anyway.

'What do you mean, touched you? You mean when he belted your bare bum?'

She twisted about, stunned that he had witnessed her nakedness. That had been a first. Before that particular incident, both she and Bill had at least been partially clothed. Uncle Jim even talked to them through the bathroom door rather than coming in.

'No, he's always doing it,' she said in a whisper, with her head down so Bill could hardly hear her.

She was so embarrassed, and had not realised her brother had viewed the latest belting and seen her unclothed. With some difficulty she told about having to get into her uncle's bed, and what he did once he assumed she was sleeping.

'And when we go to town ...'

Bill interrupted her. She was obviously getting upset so he just told her that things would soon be all right. No other comment seemed appropriate right then. They stood and balanced on the fallen trunk. It was an easy step to the next one which lay at an angle across the others. Kitty had no more she wanted to say anyway, so they made their way along its length, working through the branches. It was a bit of a challenge for they were, after all, some five or six feet above the ground.

'Bill!!!'

It was more a scream than a shout and he whirled about, thinking she had fallen through.

Uncle Jim had found them and was already charging his way along the fallen tree trunk. Until then he had been sneaking along quietly, but had no reason to be silent now. With big steps he had crashed his way though the foliage at ground level, then leapt up onto the solid trunks.

'And what do you think you're up to, eh? Just wait 'til I get my hands on you, you bloody little time-wasting brats,' he panted menacingly. 'My God, you're in for it this time. You think you've had hidings in the past, well we'll see how you fare in a minute.'

He was breathing heavily, struggling with the branches, and having difficulty steadying himself as the trunk began to sway under his added weight. Kitty was right behind Bill as they forced themselves past the last of the branches, thankful they had the advantage of smaller frames. It would be more difficult for him to move through, but even so, that final portion was hell as the gap closed between them. Every branch reached out, grasping at them in a deliberate attempt to halt their progress. He was still gaining. They could hear and feel his presence as he deliberately rocked the trunk in an effort to slow their escape, and heard his laboured breath only yards behind. They visualised outstretched hands right there behind their shoulders. Reaching. Grasping. Almost touching them.

That last leap to the ground was a relief, and immediately they sensed the chance for freedom was still with them.

'Run... run for your life!'

'Wait Bill, don't leave me behind!'

With the slope ahead of them they sprinted away, disregarding any thrashing branches that flayed unprotected faces and bare arms. Cruel tree roots spread out across the path, lying poised and ready to trip the unwary. When they felt like slowing, the sound of heavier footsteps thumping the ground behind urged them on again. They got louder and closer on the long clear stretches, growing fainter on the twisting bits where agility gave them an edge.

The ground levelled out with no clear route to follow, then fell away once more. They were disoriented.

'I'm exhausted.' She choked the words, and followed them with a whimpering, 'Let's give up?'

'No!' Bill was determined they could do it, and he searched the ground ahead for the correct track. Holding hands, and more dragging her than running together, they fled further down the hill and soon disappeared from sight.

It had taken Dwyer extra time to thrash the bulk of his body through those last few branches and reach firm ground. Not sure if he had lost them at that point, he stood momentarily cursing and panting. But the squealing he finally heard way off out of sight enabled him to get his bearings, and during the next twenty minutes or so there were two or three occasions when he almost had them again. But now it was silent and he paused once more, squatting out of sight straining to detect the sounds he needed to hear.

Bill and Kitty rested too, but very briefly. It was really only a breath-catching stop, then off. After ten minutes of running they collapsed to the ground again. And this time it was ominously quiet. No sound of bird life. Not even a rush of wind whipping the branches. Then they heard him again. Charging forward, crashing a passage through the undergrowth somewhere off behind them. Dwyer was making his own track, not caring about any noise he made. He hoped he could flush them out, and was just as determined not to give up. It was time to change direction and tactics. They ran, and at the same time looked for a suitable hiding place. Somewhere Uncle Jim would least expect. They were lucky the ground was fairly open beneath these trees. It was easier to run. But then again, it was easier for him too.

'Wait.'

It was the top of a sudden drop into a stream bed, and Bill stopped Kitty suddenly. There was no noise behind at the moment, for somehow they had got sufficiently ahead of him. Bill threw his jersey down into the stream where it landed on the rocks. He dumped Kitty's at the top not far from them.

'Wait here.'

Sliding down the bank he then scrabbled his way back up, leaving plenty of evidence he had been down there. Bill was using his own hunting skills now. He knew Uncle Jim would be on the look-out for a sign. Knew how he would be thinking. This chase would be bringing the stalker out in Jim Dwyer.

'What are you doing?' Kitty asked, reaching to pick up her clothing.

'Leave it and follow me,' he ordered. 'He'll think we went down there, dropping our stuff as we ran.'

She understood immediately, and they melted into the undergrowth, moving silently off in the opposite direction. Suddenly there was an eerie quietness in the bush again. It was easier for them to move now without the bulk of additional belongings. And with the pressure off, they could concentrate on moving quietly rather than dodging branches and other obstacles. Dwyer had also slowed. He too was aware of changes up ahead. He had heard nothing of them for a while now but felt sure he was still on their trail. This was confirmed some moments later when he came across the slope leading down to the stream and picked up the discarded item of clothing. He could see where they had slid into the water, and saw other clothing down there too. He stepped forward, feeling sure he was closing in on them now. Dwyer laughed out loud at their panic, at how in their desperation to escape they had dropped stuff and slithered through mud and water in their fear of him. Like a lithe animal he leapt down the bank and stood in the stream amongst slimy brown rocks. Water cascaded over his boots, and the cool of the stream bed was a welcome relief after the last hour's chase. Above, and in every direction, a tangle of supplejack surrounded him. He expected to hear crashing noises as the kids pushed their way noisily through yet another net of vines, but the chatter and gurgle of water over rocks drowned out everything and he cursed aloud. He needed to be higher, realised it quickly, and headed for the other side. But then Dwyer hesitated and took a deliberate step back. Something was out of place. And then a cruel sneer formed on his face.

'Crafty little bastards,' he thought to himself. If they were in such a hurry, they would have splashed their way through this stream and out the other side. He looked carefully at all rocks above the water line, noting how they had remained dry. Even the easiest exit showed no sign of disturbance. He stepped back from the flow, slowly retracing the last few steps. Looking for the little brats' true route. There was no evidence. Clambering back to the top again, he stayed down on all fours studying the obvious, and then carefully gazed back behind him at the least likely options. Listening as a calm descended on the area. A calm accentuated by the ghostly mist which once again drifted through moss-covered trees. The silence deepened, with not even the sound of insect or bird life evident. Dwyer rose and ran forward, hoping to flush the kids out, but then squatted again and remained in a crouch to lessen his chances of detection. There was nothing to indicate the whereabouts of hunter or quarry. In fact, it was frighteningly quiet.

Some short distance off, Bill and Kitty had stopped and lain down, stretching out amongst a dense patch of fern. Kitty lay with her hands over her ears as if the blocking out of noises would help make him move on. Bill strained to listen. He had heard Dwyer crashing about, and the direction the noise had come from indicated his ploy had only given them extra time rather than fooling the man completely. With Kitty curled up beside him, neither was going to chance a reassuring look, and remaining motionless was the best option. It was uncomfortable, but neither dared shift position. Half an hour passed. At one point they had the feeling he had located them, and was creeping closer, step by step. Kitty sensed it first. Her eyes caught those of Bill's, but his expression convinced her to wait. They held their breath. It was like a game of 'Hide and Seek' gone wrong, with awful consequences.

A noise off to the right gave them both a start, and Kitty responded with a loud whisper. Perhaps too loud.

'Come on, let's go the other way.'

'No wait,' Bill hissed firmly.

There was something about the sound that was not right. There it was again. A noise that was out of place. A piece of stick perhaps. Something being thrown. It had to be Uncle Jim. But he was not where the noise was. He was elsewhere. It was a trick.

'Shhh,' Bill whispered gently, 'stay very still.'

There was nothing for a long time. Bill thought of those movies when someone came out of hiding too soon. He and Kitty would wait longer. They had time. It just needed more patience than usual. A further, painfully long twenty minutes passed. Then they heard it. The scuff of clothing as he stood up from a position quite a bit closer to them than expected. Dwyer was moving again. He shuffled on past. Only a matter of yards away. They could so easily have jumped up earlier and run straight into his arms. He had failed to fool them. Their patience had beaten his patience, but where was he now?

Again they waited. Then some minutes later, rising cautiously, ready to sprint if need be, they crept away from the thick scrub-like foliage and into a bit of a clearing. Not far away something attracted Bill's attention, and once he felt it safe to do so, they again linked hands and headed quickly in that direction. It looked like sheets of corrugated iron and seemed a better place to hide.

CHAPTER 9

• • • • • • •

In the moments beforehand any noise from the struggling plane would have been barely audible. Had anyone been out there long ago, on that night back in the 1930s or 1940s, they would have had difficulty identifying the sound. Detecting the direction it was coming from would have been an impossibility, for a wild storm was raging. It was an unforgiving mountain range, and an area that seemed to attract the dirtiest of weather. Mist or wind, probably both, were always effective in muffling distant sounds. A howling wind or an engine? A plane straining to gain height? Who could tell? Had the pilot been a little higher, or the load lighter, the outcome would have been different. But neither was the case, and the end result was inevitable. It must have become very clear in those final moments that they were never going to clear the ridge. In desperation the pilot attempted to turn back. Or so the searchers assumed when they found the remains some weeks later. In a valley as narrow as this one, it must surely have been an action of last resort. Rock walls drawing the plane closer with almost magnetic attraction. Clutching fingers as the highest branches touched then ripped at its underbelly, and then the ground almost leaping up to meet the aircraft. Finally, with both engines screaming, the noise would have stopped abruptly, the power of the storm swallowing all further sounds.

A resulting scar in the landscape remained apparent for a long time. But then many months after the crash, branches and larger broken limbs began to give birth to new spring growth. Restoration of the upper canopy of foliage commenced, and the wound in the hillside slowly healed. At ground level things happened at a different pace. Once the trees had closed over, the normal internal climate was restored. While some ground level regeneration was hampered by deer and other animal activity, soon vines and ferns took hold, filling in all the voids. Pieces of metal, haphazardly strewn about as if by a giant hand, were soon barely recognisable as being the remains of a plane. Lichen spread like a disease over the broken carcass attempting to disguise the metallic intruder lying so obviously out of place amongst the natural greenery. Time passed, and the plane became fully camouflaged by a process of decay and regrowth. A process as natural in the bush as the passing of seasons. Within a year it was difficult to pick out even the structural bones of wreckage. And with the passing of a decade or more, the disintegration of most parts had been completed. Eventually all that was left were a few flat sheets of slimy green fuselage and a heavy silence.

• • • • • • •

Keeping as low as possible, they made their way quickly across the gap with the minimum of sound. The open space amongst some larger trees marked the head of a gully which then dropped away steeply below them and out of sight. At first the sheets of metal took the form of an old car, but they knew that could not be possible. Little of the plane was left, and it needed a fair bit of imagination to make out the basic shape of its body.

'What is it?'

'A plane, Kitty, but it's been here for years. It must have been found and partially salvaged long ago, 'cause the guts of it is missing and the rest has rotted away. It'll have to do for the night.'

It was not because the remains afforded any shelter, but more because it was getting late and there was no real point in trying to distance themselves further from Dwyer.

'Better to let him move away from us,' Bill said, as they settled down in as comfortable a spot as could be found. 'It'll be dark in less than an hour anyway.'

It was the smell of cigarettes that gave him away. He was not smoking at that particular moment, but the stink of past fags hung on his clothing as always. That pungent aroma of roll-your-owns, indicating that once again he was close by. Bill had noticed it first. The smell got stronger as each minute passed, and he alerted Kitty with a gentle touch of his hand. They half-rose in readiness. He was coming, but they could not tell from which direction. It was a case of being prepared for the very worst. They stood tall now, standing back to back watching, listening, sniffing the air the way Holloway's dogs did. Flicking their eyes towards every snap of a twig. Doing anything to give them an advantage.

There was no doubting Dwyer's hunting ability. Having established he had somehow moved ahead, the man began working his way back, circling and circling and narrowing down the options until he was pretty certain of the general area they were in. He remained crouched now on higher ground, looking down through the bush. It had not taken him long to scan the area and identify two or three potential locations. As yet he had not pinpointed their exact position, but he had heard them, and sensed roughly where they should be. He needed another mistake on their part before, with natural cat-like stealth, he could move again.

Dwyer had not noticed the plane, but that was hardly surprising in the failing light. There were really only a few pieces left, together with the odd sheet-metal panel half-covered with rotting leaves on the ground. One virtually had to be standing on the spot to recognise the wreckage for what it was. Possibly others had passed this way over the years and had also been unaware of the crash site. His eyebrows lifted at the sound of her whispering voice carrying clearly across the space between them, breaking the silence. It was all he needed. The creases of satisfaction around his eyes were the only indication of life on an otherwise expressionless face.

He moved closer. Slowly, on all fours at first. Then like a committed animal he surged forward, charging.

It was Bill's turn to squeal this time, and it appeared to give Dwyer great delight to hear the note of fear in the boy's voice. He came crashing through the tangle of vines between him and the kids. No longer caring about noises or obstacles, he could see them and they could see him. He chuckled loudly, knowing they could hear his cruel laughter. Neither moved at first. They appeared stuck to the spot. Mesmerised. Only a few final yards and he would reach them. With one last lunge forward, his boot connected with the thing that had first attracted the children to the site — a panel of lichen and moss-covered aluminium sheeting. He could not have chosen a more slippery foothold had he tried. With momentum too great, and with both feet sliding from beneath him, Dwyer skidded, lost his balance and fell heavily.

'Shit,' he shouted, falling flat on his back and rolling awkwardly in the opposite direction.

It was all they needed. Dwyer lay winded and disorientated, and in that fleeting moment, having gathered their own senses, they once again ran for their lives. Neither could make out his words. They just ran, knowing their very survival depended on it. But for that piece of fuselage, he would have had them for sure that time.

'He wants to kill us,' sobbed Kitty.

'Just run and keep running.'

It was well dark when they slowed, but they knew this time they had finally given him the slip. That night the distant lights of one of the towns twinkled invitingly. The kids could just make them out before a heavy shower of rain obliterated the view completely. Bill was encouraged by the thought that help was close by, and it was this confidence that turned his attention to more pressing matters. Shelter.

'I'm sure we've left him miles behind us now. Especially with that last twisty bit down the stream.'

Bill smiled to himself. No one measured distance in the bush in miles, although Kitty would not have known that. Distance from one point to another in this type of terrain was always expressed in hours. But it hardly mattered. Both forms of measurement were as important on this occasion.

'I hope he's lying with a broken leg,' Kitty wished out loud.

Eventually they climbed out of the water, and made their way through and beyond a dense clump of tree ferns to an ideal spot in which to hole up. Bill left Kitty with their things and, dragging a stick behind him, made his way back in the dark. Feeling his way ahead, he located the punga patch and cut the greenery easily with his knife. Not wanting any damage to alert his Uncle Jim, he took care to remove only one branch from each fern. With arms full of the stuff he had collected, Bill followed the scratch mark he had left in the dirt and soon found Kitty crouching a hundred yards or so away in the semi-darkness. A makeshift framework from branches was all he had time for, on top of which they both heaped the fronds. What was left over went inside. It was rough and low, but cozy and dry. Just what they needed, and even from a distance of only three or four yards, difficult to detect as a hiding place.

Kitty and Bill crawled in, snuggled up, and at last felt quite safe. It was about all they could do, because despite initial thoughts their bivouac proved to be scratchy and not the most pleasant of places to spend a night. And besides, every snapping branch or unusual night-time noise alerted them to potential danger. Frequently throughout those very early morning hours, Bill found himself raised on an elbow peering out into the black and holding his breath to maximise his sense of hearing, but eventually finding there was nothing to hear or fear.

CHAPTER 10

The day dawned bleak and cold. Only a light drizzle now. Mostly mist. Wet bush has a smell of its own, and it was that dank pong of rotting vegetation that filled their nostrils. With some difficulty, pond-sized mud-holes were negotiated. Tracks in general always seemed to pick a route through the boggiest areas, and everywhere there was the sight, sound and feel of water. It was a case of gingerly brushing aside branches heavy with the previous night's rain, although there was really no point in doing so. Both were already soaked and feeling thoroughly miserable. Initially they crunched noisily through frosty portions of the track, keen to get out on the road. Then, thinking better of it, they agreed to keep to those parts where no prints would be left. Some of the puddles had iced over and held their weight when tested.

Once out on the gravel road, Bill estimated a five mile walk lay ahead of them to where they had seen the previous night's lights. This end of the road told a story of its own — beer cans and the skid marks of joy-riders. Obvious signs of an evening's entertainment by at least one car-load of louts. Rubbish and broken bottles lay haphazardly discarded in the grass. Fish and chip papers everywhere. The thought of food brought on those hunger pangs again. Kitty was so wet, her hands were blue with cold, yet despite all this there was still an inclination to pause and admire the surrounding sights. These hedges must have been infested with a million spiders. Webs heavy with dew danced in the light breeze. They sparkled like jewels and were the only indication there was a sun somewhere, doing its best to clear a path through an otherwise misty morning. It was easier to climb the gate rather than get the chain and catch to work. Frozen fingers were unable to move this morning.

Outside the first farm entrance they came to a rural postie was manoeuvring his van. It was his early run delivering milk and morning papers, and a welcome face.

'Fancy meeting you two so far from home,' he called out. 'It's my last delivery, so I'm heading back now if you're wanting a lift anywhere.'

'Yes please, Mr Johnston.'

They really had no idea where they were, so it was so good to see someone they knew.

'You both staying over here or what?'

Kitty started to explain, and after hearing a little of what had been going on he suggested a visit to someone who might be able to help. Later Bill guessed he had put it that way so as not to frighten them. Mr Johnston had kids of his own, and was not at all happy about finding these two so far away and obviously on the run. From what little he had heard, this was something the authorities needed to be involved in. No doubt he would hear more in the way of detail at some later stage. For now, though, he wanted them to be in more suitable surroundings.

They pulled up at the police station half an hour later and the trio was ushered into a waiting-room. The kids listened to him in the next room explaining as best he could to the officer in charge. They soon realised they had come out on Kaipaitangata Road on the outskirts of Carterton. Less than ten miles as the crow flies from where they had entered the Tararuas but twenty miles by road. It was lucky the postie had such a long mail route.

'I thought we'd have come out at Otaki Forks on the other side of the range,' Bill whispered to Kitty.

Once Mr Johnston had left, the policeman told them he needed to have a talk, but would first organise a change of clothing. A lady living next to the station arrived soon after that, and it was arranged she would take care of them.

'You two dears come with me. There's a nice hot bath waiting and we'll get those clothes of yours dried too.'

They followed her down the path and into a nice-smelling kitchen. Home-made bread and other aromas. Bill sat by the fire with a hot drink. Coffee, and more if he wanted it. Kitty was whisked away to the bathroom. Later the lady was overheard talking to her husband in the garden.

'You should have seen the state of that poor girl's body. She's had a beating. Welts like you'd never believe.'

A different constable came into the living room later, and they were left with him to tell what had been happening. It was all written down. It took a while, and Kitty felt embarrassed once again. Between the two of them enough facts came out. He said they would be paying Dwyer a visit but, more importantly, assured them they would not be returned to his care. More appropriate arrangements were already underway. Kitty asked if they could stay with the lady who was looking after them now, but it appeared unlikely. They were allowed to stay the night, though, and most of the next day. She spoke very kindly to them and her husband was pleasant too. It was a change to feel safe and wanted once more.

Jim Dwyer had gone. When the police arrived two days later it was obvious from the state of his home that no one had been in residence overnight. Cold ashes in the fireplace and milk that was going off, a clear enough indication of an absent owner. Also, the front door had not been latched properly and an evening's rain had left damp patches inside. They waited for an hour then drove away. A return visit later in the day also proved fruitless. Neighbours were unable to help when questioned, and in the end the farmer from whom the family had rented the property told police he would wait a week then look at putting someone else in there. He was more concerned he would be out of pocket with unpaid rent than anything else. No doubt a sale of what little furniture had been left would help recoup any loss of income.

Word got around pretty quickly after the Wilson kids left the area. Of course there were those parents who claimed they had never been comfortable with the situation from the outset. The usual group outside Smetherton's dairy was talking again. It was the only subject for a while.

'Fancy an older man looking after those kids without some other family member stepping in and taking over. It was a disgraceful arrangement.'

'I don't think the Wilsons had any other family in New Zealand, did they?'

Others were openly surprised, and many steadfastly refused to accept that what supposedly had been happening, 'virtually on their doorstep', had any factual base.

In the months that followed there were rumours, the most outrageous being that the kids had been murdered in their sleep and their bodies disposed of down a disused well on the property. There were many arguments too, and just as many 'informed' people contributing to the stories doing the rounds.

'It's all crap, we've heard from reliable sources that Jim Dwyer was spotted dragging two heavy sacks and a spade off into the bush. Three or four people saw it happening weeks ago.'

'Well I don't know,' contributed yet another, 'that chap Dwyer had a bit of history with the Australian police didn't he? His wife died too. Probably poisoned a number of people over the years, and just clever enough to remain ahead of the law. In fact, it wouldn't surprise me if the kids had stumbled onto his secret and had become victims as a result. Got drowned for their trouble, I'd say.'

It got to a point where the headmaster had to speak rather sternly to his pupils in the hope the message would also get back to adult rumour-mongers in the community. There was to be no more of the silliness.

'It's more than likely Jim Dywer has left the district and possibly the country by now,' he said. 'What's more important,' he added in a gentle voice, 'is the fact the authorities have confirmed both children have been placed in safe care and are none the worse for their recent experiences. And we should all be thankful for that.'

Everyone was encouraged to get on with his or her own affairs, and within weeks the matter had effectively been brushed aside. When a story started a month later that Dwyer had been seen over the hill working with one of the Rimutaka railway tunnel gangs, it was one that did not last long. It may have been true, but by now no one really cared.

The kids were informed they were to spend time apart and this news came as a bit of a blow. Single sex accommodation was immediately available, but it was hoped the splitting of the brother and sister arrangement might only be a temporary one.

'Until suitable foster care is organised,' the policeman advised.

No one seemed to know what the future held for the children, and all too soon Kitty had been whisked away. It was a bus trip to Dannevirke and then on by train to Palmerston North for her. Apparently there was a convent in Pascal Street with a spare bed, and Bill was advised he could write if he wanted to. Some time after her departure he realised they had not even said a proper goodbye. He had no idea when he might see his sister again and it had not occurred to the authorities, let alone the kids, that some years might pass before their next meeting.

A constable they had both met earlier in the day came for Bill mid-afternoon. He enjoyed being in the police car, and pleased also to be staying in the vast Wairarapa area close to the mountain range which stretched itself out beside him like a sleeping giant. Once the sun dropped beyond the Tararuas, however, the wrinkles and creases of the range's skin-like surface melded into one long dark shape and the afternoon grew colder. Towards the day's end, Bill found himself being led by the hand up a meandering driveway. A light covering of gravel meant each footstep made a crunching noise. It sounded as if they were marching.

From the outside, the orphanage was not as he expected it would be. He had envisaged a grim place, but this one had lots of well cared-for gardens and newly-painted buildings. It was surrounded by a high fence, and looked more like a hospital to him. An impressive front door was pinned open with highly polished brass hooks, inviting entry to a dark corridor. Ahead of them there was a waiting area near the main office, and it was here he sat while the policeman went off to make enquiries on Bill's behalf. The long narrow corridor resounded to the measured steps of people in hard shoes way off in the distance. Apart from that it was awfully quiet. Bill felt it was a place where it was best you whispered rather than spoke aloud.

The constable returned, and they were eventually ushered into the office where a Mr Wilton introduced himself. He was the Director. An older man who spoke softly in a manner that immediately put people at ease. The way he described the place made Bill feel he would enjoy being there for his short visit. Standing with his back to the window, it was hard to make out the man's features against a brighter background. Mr Wilton was not a large person, but his suit was too big. Even Bill could tell it was a poor fit. They all talked for a while, and despite Bill's ease, he found it difficult to provide more than one-word answers to any of the questions. There were some papers to complete. It was the first time he had ever had to sign his name, and had problems managing the fat fountain pen. Perhaps his hand was too small, or maybe his limited schooling to date was showing.

Eventually the policeman wished him good luck for the future and shook his hand as if farewelling a 'grown up'. He left soon after that, strolling off with Mr Wilton through the front door and on towards the car. They talked for a while out of Bill's hearing.

'He and his sister have had a bit of a harsh time these past couple of years it seems. Bill needs some gentle fatherly attention and a fresh start in life.'

'Well, he'll certainly get that here. We don't believe in corporal punishment as you know. We never have problems with any of our boys,' Mr Wilton stated emphatically.

Bill looked around, feeling like a dwarf in the high-walled office. He wondered aloud how anyone could reach books on the top of the 'floor to ceiling' shelving. Large paintings strategically placed on all four walls looked old and interesting, but it was the high-backed leather chair that took most of his attention. Fifty eight brass studs around the leather squab he was sitting on. He had counted them twice until finally distracted by the sound of voices outside. Bill moved to the window.

A group of kids his own age were kicking the hell out of a football and revelling in the mud. Not team against team, but each on his own, laughing and pushing. They looked a friendly bunch.

'You'll meet up with them later, but first we'll find Matron', came Mr Wilton's voice from behind him.

He was introduced to Matron, but immediately forgot her name as an armful of replacement clothing was thrust at him, and he followed her quickly to his new bed in the dormitory. There were twelve single beds. Six to each side of the room. Everything was very tidy, and once he had organised his stuff in drawers allocated to him, she took him on to her dispensary to fix up medical records. He was weighed, measured and generally checked over. Teeth, hair, the works.

'Just looking for nits and other nasties,' she said, 'but you're not too bad, Bill.'

When they got back to the room most of the others were there too. Matron introduced him to the rabble, as she called them, and showed him the chart on the wall by the door. It listed House Rules. A bell in the distance announced dinnertime and a mad rush ensued. Matron left him to join the group, watching as he was enveloped into their fold. The pack raced down the stairs, despite the 'no running' rule, and lined up outside the dining room. This was a new beginning, and somehow Bill felt he would long remember the distinctive smell of boiled cabbage. Some boys were still complaining about that morning's lukewarm water in the showers.

'That's why you're only allowed three minutes in the shower,' one said. 'It's on the Rules chart.'

Another voice said they were restricted to only three pieces of toilet paper too. 'One up, one down, and one for a polisher.' Everyone laughed and he realised his new mates were just joking. During the meal there were many questions, and it became clear others were staying here for a whole variety of reasons. It made no sense to give all his details, so he just said his parents had died in a car crash and that was that.

Bill suffered badly from the change of diet, and a few days later found himself confined to bed. Outside, the wind blew in strong gusts so as it turned out he was probably in the best place after all. Poplar trees lining the driveway bent and strained in the storm, and sheets of rain lashed at the orphanage windows.

Everyone else was spending the day in the dining area playing cards and he felt as if he had been quarantined. It was a day that passed very slowly. Matron had given him some evil-tasting medicine earlier and her footsteps could again be heard in the passage. Pretence of sleep seemed his best line of defence, and that was how she found him when tip toeing into the dormitory. Nothing was said. He could feel her eyes on him for some time as she searched for the slightest indication he was faking it. She stood motionlessly for a while with bottle and teaspoon in hand, waiting for him to open his eyes, but eventually leaving him to doze away the day. He smiled inwardly. She had obviously not come up against someone with his depth of patience before.

His mates joined him mid-afternoon when they got bored, and each tried to outdo the other with stories of past adventures or things they knew that others might not. One boy's experience of firing a rifle prompted Bill to pass on Uncle Jim's clever knack of lighting a fire, and they listened spellbound to his explanation. Over past weeks, thoughts of Uncle Jim had slipped well into the background to the point he now felt he could speak openly of some special moments he had enjoyed. It was still there, though, the hatred and the loathing. Just tucked away. Bill was determined not to feel out of place with his friends, so brought to the fore those memories of a few good times when Jim Dwyer had stimulated his young mind.

'What I do with my rifle,' he announced, as if speaking from personal experience, 'is this.'

They gathered closer, sapping up any knowledge he had to give. Intrigued that one of their number had actually owned a rifle.

'First, you prepare your fire by gathering all the wood you need. No point going off for more if it's only just going. Because,' he added with a serious note to his voice and an appropriate pause for effect, 'ten bob to a knob of that other stuff, the bloody thing will go out.'

He was mimicking his uncle now and even had the mannerisms right.

'Then you get all the tinder ready.'

'What the hell's that?'

'It's stuff that will catch alight easily right at the start. Like the smallest of dry twigs and dusty dry bark. Even dry fluff out of your pockets. And you've got to arrange the small stuff carefully so it doesn't collapse and crowd itself. A fire needs air.'

'But what about the rifle? You said you used a .303 to light the fire,' one of them enquired.

'I'm getting to that part. What you do once you're ready is take the end out of the bullet.'

He paused again, looking about him and beyond for uninvited guests, as if it was a special secret for only this group to know. They huddled closer.

'The projectile,' someone contributed.

'Yes, that bit. You might have to jam the bullet in the wrong end of the barrel, and work it back and forth to loosen it up. Then you carefully pour half the powder out onto the stuff you've set up for the fire, because when that's lit it'll really flare up and help things along. Next you tear a bit of material off your shirt, just a small piece, rub a bit of powder on that and stuff it in where the projectile was. Having dug a cavity in the ground so you don't lose it, you fire the rifle into the hole.

The kids surrounding him looked at one another with amazement, and then leaned forward again hanging on his every word.

'This is the part where you have to work really quickly. With only a half charge of powder the rag shouldn't bounce away, and will still be smouldering when you pick it out of the hole. Sometimes you have to carefully blow on it to keep the thing glowing, but speed is essential in getting it to your pile of small stuff. That's the key.'

They were not all his own words. Much of it was a direct copy of his uncle's instruction many months earlier.

'Just chuck it in there and it's away,' he summed up.

Once again he paused for effect.

'So that's what I do when I want a fire,' Bill said, sitting back with a content look on his face.

From that point on the boys looked at Bill through different eyes. It seemed he had done the things they could only dream of.

The late afternoon was wasting away, and Bill was feeling good enough for a boisterous pillow fight and to be thinking of dinner too. There was still a furious storm outside, and during one particular blast they gathered together at the window to watch as the wind continued to strip trees of any remaining foliage and scatter leaves and rubbish. A large pool of water had accumulated on the lawn. From the looks in their eyes it was obvious they were hoping it would still be there in the morning. Funny how much enjoyment boys get from messing about in water. The bell was a long time coming, but eventually the sound signalled the usual race down the corridor.

• • • • • • •

Bill would not forget his twelfth birthday. They were treated to a trip away on that day. Not because it was his birthday of course, but because it was the opening day of the tunnel under the Rimutakas just south of them. The ninth of November 1955. They went by bus over the winding road and joined hundreds of other vehicles on the Wellington side of the range. Mr Holland, Prime Minister of the day, would be attending they were told, and also the Minister of Railways, a Mr McAlpine. It was an important occasion. Their group arrived at the Mangaroa entrance and was allowed up on the back of a truck for a better view. It was a great vantage spot from which to see the pomp and ceremony. Mr Holland cut the ribbon and officially opened the line forming part of a fourteen mile deviation.

'It will effectively shorten the old route by eight miles,' he announced, 'and allow diesel locomotives to haul 600 tons of freight instead of the sixty-five ton restriction on the mountain line.'

The new diesels looked so modern beside the old-fashioned Fell engines.

It was a good day's outing, and the boys all felt special being allowed to watch from their makeshift viewing platform. Bill looked down on the sea of faces. There were hundreds of people, most wearing hats. Off to the left stood groups of railways officials, and behind them dozens of employees and contractors, many of whom had been involved in the digging of this tunnel. From amongst the crowd an individual stared intensely at the school group. Bill felt the man's eyes drawing him in, and he focused on his face. His initial reaction was that it was simply a stranger, but then the hair on Bill's neck prickled. Mutual recognition dawned on them both. They stared long and hard. Bill's gaze dropped first and when he looked back Jim Dwyer had gone. Melting back within the ranks and unlikely to be seen again. Bill felt his presence, though, and remained on guard at all times.

While it was a great occasion, and an important day, it was good to get back on the bus. They headed home an hour or so later after stopping briefly in Featherston. There had been talk that one of the old engines being replaced would probably end up being mounted in a local park there. But it was only when closer to home that Bill found he was finally able to relax.

The months passed and Bill and a couple of the others were eventually shifted on to Palmerston North. Another welfare-type home not far from the stock car track. They could hear the noise and smell the special fuel being used.

Palmerston North Boys' High was where he was to finish off his schooling, so the move made sense. The large college was spread out over flat grounds, and some of the teachers looked as if they had been there forever. A well-worn path past the corrugated iron-clad swimming pool fence to a small shop on Rangitikei Street enabled students the freedom to buy food, sweets and drinks during the lunch hour. Bill was quickly absorbed into the gang of older boys who attended the college and were allowed to walk the distance from the home to school. It only took them twenty minutes or so, and they also had permission to forgo cut lunches and buy their own once a week. Thursday was their special day.

A muddy path linked the pool with a tar-sealed area between buildings where outside assemblies were often held. It ran past a row of old villa-style homes, and you could look into the dirty back yards. These homes on Wellesbourne Street had been hidden for years by a row of trees but were now open to the school's playing field. They were pretty derelict properties. Nevertheless, people did live there, and the boys would sometimes see some activity that confirmed occupancy. Most students did not give the properties a second glance, but the dwellings meant something to Bill. Perhaps it was the age of the occupants, or that the style of house was similar to the home he had left behind. Whatever the reason, each day he passed by he was reminded of those difficult years spent in similar housing with Uncle Jim.

CHAPTER 11

Martin Foulds lay in the sun and looked at the ruins in the paddock beyond him. Not much to see now, but he was aware of the significance of the site. A piece of New Zealand's wartime history. Something that had fascinated him when he had first learned of it as a younger man. He had heard of it, but had never seen the place. It looked as if nothing much had changed over the years. After travelling extensively overseas, and having seen similar relics of the past, he thought it a shame that a prisoner of war camp for Japanese soldiers just outside Featherston was something today's commuters simply rushed past with little thought for the brief skirmish and resultant loss of life. Just another bit of farmland to them. Just a few bits of concrete in the grass, and a vague indication of where buildings had once stood. Not a lot to see. Not even a plaque to mark the spot. Perhaps someone would do something about that in the years to come.

He had decided to try his luck back here in New Zealand again, and the trip had been an easy one so far for someone travelling as lightly as he was. No real destination. No family really, and anyone he had known years back had probably moved on long ago or died. Bit of a long shot expecting to find work and to catch up with past acquaintances, but the decision had been made months ago and here he was. Australia had become a bit seedy he had thought. Well the suburbs he had been frequenting had 'gone down hill' anyway, and he was not one to hang around if things were not safe or to his liking. He would hardly describe himself as being cowardly. More a cautious soul, he thought smugly.

The sun beat down mercilessly, and he raised himself up at the sound of another vehicle. They tended to get along quite briskly on this bit of road. A nice long straight before reaching the bridge over the Tauherenikau river. An earlier lift had told him to try the pub there. The 'Tin Hut' just outside the race track gates. Great place for a pub dinner and somewhere to put your head down, he had been told. Even if it was a night in their wood shed. This car was just toddling along so he had a better chance of waving it down. Its worn engine left a smear of bluish smoke behind it, hanging in the stillness of the day. Foulds watched the Morris Minor struggling in its bid to maintain a decent pace on what was otherwise an easy stretch of road. He had had one of them himself as a younger man, and remembered with a smile the day a stone had busted one of its headlights and blown a fuse. A temporary repair with a piece of silver paper from his cigarette pack carefully wound around a match stick had been sufficient to get the remaining light working again. He had shoved it in where the failed fuse had been, then forgotten it and driven for months before selling the car, complete with makeshift electrics. Foulds stepped out from the grass verge and raised his hand.

Ever since seeing the boy a couple of months earlier, Dwyer had a feeling the net was closing on him. He assumed the kid had alerted the authorities, and that it would only be a matter of time before he was pulled in for questioning. For that reason alone he had decided to move on. No point in staying in a job where you either had friends or enemies. There seemed to be no mid-point amongst the railyard workers. You were either regarded as being 'in' or 'out'. No half-way measures there. It was common knowledge that shunting accidents had been arranged for those who had fallen foul of others. Better not to risk it, he had decided. If the word was out that someone was on a wanted list, then it was unlikely that person would be free for long. Despite an unwritten law that everyone closed ranks in times of strife and protected one another, there was always someone who would speak up. Especially if there was a 'quid' to be earned.

'Abusive activities?' he stated with surprise. 'What utter crap.' He mouthed the denial. Practised the words for when his time came. His brow furrowed, for it was not just his dealings with the Wilson kids that worried him. He could explain that away easily enough. It had not been his choice. He had been forced into an unexpected role as a temporary father, and it was he who had suffered as a consequence. They were unruly kids, and a belting or two was justified in the circumstances. Nor was it his past in Australia that worried him. They could never pin anything on him from that far back. No, it was more his activities in the years that followed that worried him most. A thorough investigation might be a bit embarrassing. No doubt there was a growing police file on him somewhere.

Dwyer had enjoyed watching children coming and going from schools in the Upper Hutt area. He had loitered near a number of them and frequented the council reserves over the years. Unfortunately he had been warned off on several occasions too, often claiming it was the young ones who wanted to stop and talk to him. He used to park down the road and wait. There were a lot of kids who would stop for a chat. Some even sat in his car and passed the time of day with him. They seemed to like him. The sweets always helped. Anyway that had been a while back now. He had ceased his activities because he felt he was 'becoming known' to the authorities.

Dwyer was driving an old bomb these days. A well-used Morris Minor, and he pulled over just ahead of the hitchhiker. He could do with some friendly conversation. His rear vision mirror had thumbprints obliterating the view. It required frequent adjustment and had slipped yet again. He moved it to the correct position, and watched as a man of similar age gathered up a small amount of luggage and ran towards the car. Dwyer reached back, slipped the catch, and in doing so confirmed his willingness to assist. The rear door was hurriedly opened from the outside, and a dusty suitcase quickly placed on the back seat.

'Thought I'd never get a lift,' said the man as he climbed in. 'Thanks very much. I'm Martin Foulds. Heading for Napier, how about you?'

'That direction anyway,' said Dwyer eyeing him carefully.

Sure he was going to Napier and well beyond. That had been his intention all along. But Dwyer was a cunning type, and cautious enough not to commit himself too early in the piece. There was always the possibility they may not hit it off. Easier to jettison a 'pain in the arse' passenger by indicating a closer destination at the outset. If things looked like they might not work out, that was. He could always review the situation later on.

The car's tyres scrabbled in loose gravel as he pulled back into the flow of traffic.

'Funny how you get great long gaps between cars and then all of a sudden a line of them like this. I've been travelling throughout Australia for the last five years or more. God, I haven't been home for must be at least eight years or so.'

'A talker,' Dwyer thought, and readied himself for a good discussion. Home was apparently somewhere in Auckland, so any distance in that direction would be useful, Foulds had indicated.

'Don't really have proper family you know. No one's actually expecting me, so it'll be a surprise for friends when I arrive. Travel tends to keep you away from family and mates. Flew into Wellington yesterday, you know. Plenty of casual work here I understand, but only if you're prepared to look for it,' he told Dwyer.

After exchanging a few pleasantries they found some common ground. Both had hunted crocs in Queensland, and even deer in these local ranges once. Foulds settled back at last and listened to Dwyer's views on hunting. He contributed only a little from then on, giving the odd nod of agreement whenever he felt it appropriate to do so. He could tell Dwyer had opinions that others may not necessarily share, and wondered whether anyone ever challenged the guy. The driver was certainly someone who liked to hear his own voice, he decided. The road was good, and with a steady speed they were able to cover a fair mileage over the next few hours. At 4.00 p.m. Dwyer enquired as to his passenger's overnight arrangements.

'Playing it by ear mate, playing it by ear.'

'I do this trip from time to time, and if I get this far then there's a shack at Pukeora I often use just this side of Waipukurau. You're welcome to stay too,' Dwyer continued. 'Ain't much, but it's shelter. The chap who lets me use it is fishing down south this time of year.'

'Thanks. Yeah thanks, mate, may as well. You're heading on for Napier tomorrow then?'

Dwyer confirmed this was his intention, and slowed the car at the next side road. They had got on okay enough, and he could do with some company overnight. Besides, his passenger had half a dozen tall bottles of Old Style Bavarian bitter with him. They looked as if they would be better with their tops knocked off.

The accommodation was just off the main road. An old shed, probably a large car-case originally. The key to the padlock was in its usual place, hidden on the tank stand, and with its iron tank full the water tasted good. However, a dozen pinprick spots weeping rusty orange streaks down its side indicated better days had long passed, and dribbling water had made the woodwork green with slime. It looked pretty fragile and unstable.

'Careful with the tap on that thing,' Dwyer warned.

Inside was pretty basic. That was about all you could say for a place like this. A simple base for hunting trips. In the late sun you could see hills, probably the Ruahines. Not as impressive as the Tararuas, they lay like a rumpled blanket cast in a northerly direction, having started where the more southerly range had ended at the Manawatu gorge. This hill country offered a different kind of hunting. Most who journeyed beyond the farmland said the terrain was easier, but pig hunting still sorted the men from the boys. Especially in those months when the range's rounded tops displayed a chilly white mantle as first evidence of winter.

Dwyer had come prepared with food for his overnight stay. He could stretch it to cover two mouths. He was familiar with the burner for heating food, and when Foulds returned with a half pot of water, Dwyer balanced it on the ancient kerosene stove with a careful hand, then slowly introduced the contents of a can of Irish stew.

'Takes about ten minutes and makes a good soup. There's some butter if you want to fix your bread. I'll put a brew on afterwards, unless you're going to do something with that beer of yours,' Dwyer hinted.

'Forgot about those,' said his new friend. 'Want one now?'

'Never been known to say "no",' Dwyer replied with a broad smile.

They drank, and smoked until well after 11.00 p.m. His passenger had a string of crude yarns, but then so too had Dwyer. As the evening progressed they flicked countless cigarette butts in the direction of the door. Most found their way out into the night. From time to time some missed the gap, and needed crushing underfoot on a floor scattered with their own debris and rubbish left by others.

'Have you heard the one about the vicar and the cucumber?' Foulds asked with a chuckle.

They were as bad as each other. Their own laughter at the crucial moment meant punchlines usually had to repeated. Some yarns he had heard already, but as far as the new ones were concerned, Dwyer doubted he would remember them in the morning. Finally it got quiet. Having exhausted their repertoires, Foulds stowed his gear back in the car and had a last pee in the bushes before turning in. Just a thin mattress each and some blankets. The warm glow faded away as the kerosene lamp was turned down for a while. And then completely off. It was pitch black. There was no illumination other than a faint moonlight through the cracks. No street lights of course. Occasionally they heard vehicles speeding past in the distance, but they were few and far between. Snoring noises from both men eventually became the only interruption to a perfect peace and quiet.

In the stillness of the night, a rat hesitantly poked its head though a gap in the woodwork. It sat twitching its nose and whiskers, and sniffed the interior's stale air in order to determine the risk of venturing further into the hut. It was attempting also to detect the smell of any food source. Eventually it scurried out across the floor, moving quickly through an accumulation of dust and discarded paper. It shuffled past a carelessly discarded fag still glowing in the corner, but finding nothing edible at ground level, moved on to look elsewhere.

When the rubbish finally erupted into flame, the snoring continued on for some time. As the fire took hold, the dry material crackled and exploded as heat and smoke rapidly intensified. And then, with a start, both men suddenly became aware of the situation. Neither stood much of a chance. In their intoxicated states, and in unfamiliar surroundings, they were at the mercy of fierce flames that blocked their only exit. Dwyer threw his blanket away from him in an eagerness to get up off the tangled bedding. With clothing strewn somewhere amongst the mess, he paused for only a fraction of a second before launching himself at where he assumed the door would be. In an instinctive move he reached for and grabbed his jacket before bursting through the flimsy panelling. With lungs crying out for clear air, and eyes streaming tears from the smoke, he crashed off into the damp undergrowth to escape the danger. His vocal companion hesitated a moment too long, and then the screaming suddenly stopped as the roof caved in amidst a shower of sparks that momentarily lit the sky. It was all over in less than twenty minutes. No one came to assist, as there was no one around. Not until later in the morning did a car eventually stop to investigate wisps of smoke from within the manuka scrub. A charred shape lay amongst the ashes, and an unmistakable smell of roasted meat hung in the stillness of the morning. The hut's only occupant was long dead and well-cooked.

Dwyer remained in the undergrowth watching from a safe distance. He had burns to his bare legs, and the cool wet grass afforded some relief. He had been coughing, but now lay quietly trying to remain undetected. He was suffering badly, but the benefit of a dry jacket keeping his upper body warm in the chill of the morning was comforting. He at least had had the sense to grab that, and later on some other gear from the vehicle. It had dawned on him within minutes of his escape that here was an opportunity to start afresh. Foulds was not going anywhere now, and from his friend's knapsack, Dwyer been able to retrieve a few essential bits and pieces. It was time to make tracks before others arrived. It was time to head for the hills where he knew he would be in his element. His injuries were not that great. He would get by and was prepared to sacrifice the car. With no family or employment ties he knew he could also spare a month or so before showing his face again. By then things should have settled down. Time for a change. And a change of identity too. Thank God Foulds' bag, left safely in the car, contained the shoes and pants he required, and in roughly his size too. Even if he had to survive on the odd 'road-kill' meal, he knew he could do it. He had served his apprenticeship long ago, and in his mind had an unequalled ability to live off the land.

To all intents and purposes, Jim Dwyer, owner of the car parked nearby, had perished in the inferno. Police records revealed a file in Dwyer's name, together with other notes bearing a notation 'unable to locate — non-urgent'. The accident was to be treated as an open and shut case. With a well-charred skeleton, but no known dental records, the evidence was nevertheless clear enough, and besides the owner had confirmed Dwyer had permission to use the site for the odd overnight stop. Papers within the file now marked 'probable offender since deceased' were unlikely to be referred to again. Mention of his death only made the local papers.

• • • • • • •

When a hand emerged from the compost heap, a houseboy's scream brought the property owners to their tip site at a run. First thoughts were that a dingo scavenging amongst the rubbish had surprised the youngster, but that was not the case as they soon found out. They were presented with something far more sinister.

A natural slope beyond the sheds had been a convenient dumping site for decades. Household refuse and bits of machinery, virtually anything that had no further use, had been discarded over the edge. From time to time there was a bit of a slump in the pile as material slipped away to the bottom of a small gully, but generally it just rotted where it lay in the Australian heat. The group stood on the lip of the drop, and stared at a spot way off in the midst of the rubble. Recently dumped stuff had caused the pile to move slightly, and this had disturbed the grisly remains. It was human alright, but meantime they would have to be satisfied with what they could see from afar. A bony claw of a hand frozen in time. Reaching out as if in some last desperate grasp for help. It had clearly been there a long time. The authorities would have to be advised of course, but it would be days before the police arrived. Everything would have to be left just as it was. In the meantime the Aboriginal workers had been spooked, and the owners expected them to go 'walk about'. In fact, as they talked matters through, some were already on their way, simply melting into the vast surrounding landscape. Any investigation and associated questioning was going to be difficult, and an uneasy quietness descended on the place as the family walked back to the house.

'That would surely date back to the Dwyer period,' someone said.

There was lengthy discussion. The group could not help but wonder at what had gone on prior to their taking ownership of the property many years earlier. In the months to follow, the official enquiry turned to New Zealand as investigators followed Jim Dwyer's trail to the Wairarapa and beyond. As a previous owner of the Australian property, there were questions they needed answers to. It was a murder enquiry, no doubt about that. The body had been trussed up in an unusual fashion. But of equal importance was a new link to another unsolved murder. The method of securing the victim's arms was similar in both cases. It was a long shot, but a skeleton found in a southern national park had a general dating that now matched Dwyer's departure from Australia. The Australian police were keen for him to be interviewed so they could perhaps eliminate him from both murder investigations.

It did not take long for their investigation file to include details of the fire just out of Waipukurau. It was clear to everyone that Dwyer had perished, and regrettably the 'Australian search' came to a natural end, leaving many questions unanswered. And so eventually it was left for the authorities to decide whether there was any merit in pursuing other avenues. They did not dwell long on the matter, concluding an unidentified native had died as a result of misadventure, and that Jim Dwyer had possibly had some unproven involvement. Perhaps the body had been that of a trespasser, and those thoughts triggered talk of a long-overdue change to finally make it a crime for land-owners to shoot natives found 'unlawfully on their land'. Investigating officers had been mindful of difficulties ahead of them with the current law, had Dwyer freely acknowledged involvement in the death of a trespasser. But would he have been able to explain the manner in which arms and legs had been restrained? As far as the other case further south was concerned, they simply had to give their prime suspect the benefit of the doubt. With no proof whatsoever that Dwyer had ever ventured beyond Sydney, what else could they do? In the end it was all conjecture. A pointless exercise in assumptions.

CHAPTER 12

Aged sixteen years, he put his schooling days behind him and stepped out into the real world. It was time to seek employment. The 1960s had arrived, and so began a different period of instability for Bill Wilson. For the first time in his life he had to fend for himself. No more clean sheets or regular hot meals. The first six months passed slowly, during which period he flitted from job to job up and down the North Island. And also from flat to flat. He found it a bit of a trial fitting in anywhere or settling into permanent work. Perhaps it was the fact he always wanted to be the one in charge that did not sit well with others. Perhaps it was simply the fact he found it difficult to trust anyone that was screwing things up for him. It always seemed easier to just move on. On reflection, a bit like his Mum and Dad's approach to life.

Bill was twenty-two years of age when he visited Palmerston North again. He had been up country for a while beforehand, working in Hamilton for the council on a contracting job he had enjoyed for a number of months. His last work for them had been cleaning and painting the municipal baths. The locals referred to them as 'the munis'. It was a job, nevertheless, and the pay had not been that bad. With a few weeks' holiday leave due to him, the decision to take a break was made and he headed back south to revisit familiar territory. The college was there on his right as he drove into town. They were painting the corrugated iron fence green. It surrounded the pool where he had learned to swim. It all looked a bit rustic compared with the munis. 'Fancy all those days at the water hole as a child, and not actually knowing how to swim,' he thought. He had learned quickly at school though, once he found he had to. Swimming sports had been compulsory. The Wellesbourne Street houses had all been demolished, and looked as if they were making way for an extension to the school grounds. Further on, the railway line no longer ran through the square at the city centre. Things had changed, and the authorities here were experimenting with a one-way vehicle system. It was a bit chaotic, even for the locals. Bill stopped for lunch at a dairy and approached a woman behind the counter who looked a bit older than him. There was something familiar about her.

'Good God, Kitty.'

'Bill?'

After all these years. Neither could believe their eyes. Surprise had been expressed, but really it was instant recognition for both of them. So good to see each other. But unexpected and awkward too. Neither made a move to hug the other or anything like that. In any event, it was a busy time of the day for her. They agreed to meet later, so Bill mucked about the city for an hour and returned when it was quieter. Kitty could not get over how much bigger he had grown — taller and more athletic, while she had stayed fairly petite and more plump than she cared for.

'You're a smoker these days, Bill,' she said, stating the obvious.

'Yeah. Hard habit to kick.'

She shouted him a coffee and they managed to talk as best they could between customer interruptions. It transpired they had both completed their schooling in Palmerston North. Just one of those flukes having never crossed paths during teenage years. Things quietened down and they were able to talk more freely.

'I'm married you know,' she said with a broad smile. 'No children yet, and Frank, well that's my husband, is a real nice guy. Really decent, Bill. You'll like him.'

'I'm pleased for you, Kitty. You deserve it. I've not got anyone special yet.'

He told her of his travels within New Zealand once he had left school, and of his various changes in employment.

'There was a period when I moved about a bit, never staying too long in any one place,' Bill continued.

'Bit of gypsy in your blood perhaps,' she giggled.

'Even did a spot of deer culling for the government for half a year. Mostly deer, but also goats and possums. Finally settled down into a permanent job up north and been there ever since. In charge of the council painters.'

'Have you ever come across Ben in your travels, or Abel?' She thought for a while before adding, 'Or that fat one? What was her name now? Bertha... that's right, Big Bertha Bradshaw. God, what a size she was, Bill.'

He said he had not, but had often wondered what had happened to their mates.

'Remember Ben's pimples,' he went on. 'Something we just accepted back then. Didn't ever give it much thought at the time, but you know if he'd ever seen a really funny film they'd probably have all popped and squirted as his face stretched with laughter.'

'Oh you're sick, Bill,' she said giving him a playful punch, and with that girlish giggle of hers again.

Although now very much a mature young woman, she had not lost those mannerisms he remembered her for. They skirted the obvious subject at first, but finally touched on the earlier years. It was obvious they would eventually reminisce about that difficult period they had both grown up through.

'You know he's dead,' she said with some contempt in her voice. It was more a statement than a question. When she saw the look of disbelief on his face, she continued. 'Thought you might have known. You know, heard about it.'

'No, nothing. What happened?'

'Burned alive, apparently. In a house fire somewhere.'

'Bloody good riddance,' he said with a look of satisfaction. 'Justice at last I suppose.'

Bill sat quietly for a moment, just thinking. It would not have surprised Kitty had he mentioned Trix at this point, for it was not uncommon for people to place more importance on cruelty to an animal as opposed to cruelty to themselves. She knew how much that puppy had meant to him.

'I've often thought of our time with him you know. I'm not sure, but just occasionally I wondered whether he had actually tried to kill me once.'

'What do you mean?'

'He was always on at me to bring in firewood. Always insisting I get stuff from the back where it was driest. He'd stacked so many weighty logs on the roof of that lean-to, it was as if he'd deliberately set it to collapse.'

Kitty sat and gazed out the window. There was nothing of interest out there but she was quiet for a long while.

'We came through it okay though,' Bill said, breaking the silence. 'No harm done, and most people's kids probably got hidings from time to time.'

He was making light of it all, even though in his own mind he could not really justify those past events. Perhaps it was because now Dwyer was dead, he could at least try to put some of those bad memories behind him. After all, they had won. Uncle Jim had lost.

Kitty was still deep in thought. She stared at her coffee. It had almost gone cold because they had chatted for so long. She held the lukewarm mug close to her chest as if it provided some form of protection.

'It wasn't that good actually, Bill,' she said, taking him into her confidence with a lowered voice.

'Being a bit younger, you probably weren't aware of what was going on all the time'.

'He belted us and shouted and made us work. And he found silly excuses so he could belt us again,' Bill said. 'Doesn't that sum it up? A whole year or more of it.'

Despite his anger, he excluded mention of the cruel fate of his puppy. He would never forget or forgive him for that, but it was not something he wanted to bring up now.

'He went further than beltings with me though, Bill. I didn't tell the police the whole story that day you know.'

Kitty reached out and touched his hand. She needed to explain. It was their first physical contact for years. Although brother and sister, there had been an immense gap in their lives. They had naturally grown apart. It was difficult for her, and he helped as best he could by not maintaining direct eye contact.

She took him back in time to those days when they were not the strangers they were today. She told him things that had been stored inside her for years. How Dwyer had been overly familiar with her. How thankfully he had not gone the whole way. Bill listened quietly. Parts of what she was saying became clear. The reason for those long periods she spent in his bedroom when he was off work with a back problem. Suddenly it was all so obvious. The reality of it dawned and it sickened him.

'It was only a matter of time before something really bad happened, Bill. But we got away. Thanks to you.'

'I had no idea,' he said. It seemed such a weak response.

As if needing to convince him further, she started to tell him of those fortnightly shopping trips that had left her feeling dirty and frightened.

'Remember the smell of Smetherton's store,' she said, 'you know, where we used to collect our fresh bread and mail.'

Bill sat back. He had forgotten, but as she spoke, he remembered some of what she was talking about and told her so. He shut his eyes, trying to visualise the interior. Initially he was unable to bring back the smell the shop, but bits of the past were starting to come to him. He thought she was switching to more pleasant memories. But with each sentence she was just proving how much she could recall. There were so many small things he had forgotten. Bill laughed when her words finally helped him remember that particular aroma.

'It always smelt of coffee grounds, sacks of grain and furniture polish. A whole mixture of pongs in one,' he announced with satisfaction.

She smiled for a moment as she reminded him also of the jangling shop doorbell. He had forgotten that too. It used to announce the arrival of yet another customer, and how they all used to say how hard it was to have just a brief visit. There had always been someone arriving or leaving. Someone to carry on a conversation with.

Kitty had remained serious throughout their discussion, flicking on and off that infectious smile of hers as the moment dictated. But gradually the smile left her face. Her overall posture changed as she slumped down into the chair with a 'far off' look in her eyes. Appearing small, fragile and drained her thoughts focused on a particular incident. It was something from years back that, at the time, had become a normal fortnightly routine for her.

'Let me tell you what used to happen,' she said. 'I sort of need to talk part of that distant life-time out of me once and for all.'

Their business in town was finished. With the morning fast passing, thoughts returned to chores waiting at home. Jim Dwyer and his girl both had things to do.

'Won't get done by themselves,' he reminded her.

'Bye Mr Smetherton. Thank you. Uncle Jim says we have to hurry.'

'Bye Kitty,' he said with a chuckle. He had always had a soft spot for that girl. Such a skinny kid and small for her age.

A bit like his own children really. So fortunate to be healthy, carefree, and living out here away from rowdy cities. All the kids around here were lucky. Even though it was sunny, there was a cold biting wind outside. It would be warmer in the car. She hesitated, though, and looked back at the shop. Mr Smetherton smiled at her and gave a cheery wave. She turned back to the car. It always took two steps. Especially with an armful of shopping. First, the narrow running board, dusty grey from the gravel road. Then onto the seat with its brown cracked surface. The leather upholstery had seen far better days in its life. She turned back to the shopkeeper, and waved to him slowly from within the car.

It was a good view from this height when she knelt up close to the glass. Although detesting the trip, there were nevertheless things to see. For a short while the countryside made her feel happy. Paddocks full of stock and gorse in full bloom made an interesting journey. The scenery passed quickly, and with farmland behind them for a while the car wound its way through a small gorge. She hoped they would keep going straight home this time. Sometimes they did. Leaning against the door, and conscious of the distance between them, Kitty dared not look in his direction. There was a place up ahead she was familiar with. There had been no other traffic, but that was not unusual on this road.

'Sit down properly,' Dwyer said suddenly, and she obeyed quickly and without comment.

A gap in the undergrowth ahead, just before the bridge, looked like the type of access you would expect would lead to a favourite fishing hole. He pulled the car off the road. The crunch of gravel had been a constant noise, but was now replaced by the scraping of branches. Lying scattered in the grass, they plucked and tugged at the vehicle as it bellied and heaved itself forward. The branches provided little resistance as it passed by, keeping to where the ground was firm and dry. It was unlikely they would get stuck. With engine off it was momentum alone that carried them on until completely out of sight of the road. The car came to a rest, and a fast-running stream nearby provided the only sound. Nothing was said for a while. They just sat in silence. It was peaceful, and despite the work she knew was waiting at home, it could have been a lovely place to picnic and waste away an afternoon. But they had been here before, and she knew there were other plans.

Physically Kitty was still immature. But she was growing up, and he had told her on a previous visit there would be differences within her she might begin to notice. Without a mother to talk to, he had taken on certain responsibilities as her guardian, and it was important he was kept informed. In any event, he would be checking her regularly. It was necessary for her health, he had lied. She dared not resist or anger him with any argument. She could not bring herself to say she was okay, that he need not concern himself with such matters. She was frightened of him.

Kitty interrupted the story briefly.

'You know what he was like, Bill, his temper and all that,' she said, forcing him to say something.

'Yes,' he said, 'I remember all right.'

'There was never anyone I dared confide in so I'd do what I was told. You know, as soon as instructed. Without hesitation. That was the way it was, back then. He didn't hurt me, just embarrassed the hell out of me. Just had a damn good look. He carried on like he was a doctor or something.'

She looked at him, searching for some understanding, then continued her story.

This was probably the fifth or sixth time they had stopped here. He left the vehicle now. Just briefly, to satisfy himself they were in fact alone. There was a look of trepidation as she pressed her face to the glass and waited for his return. He circled around, and came back from another direction. Startling her as he pushed his way noisily through the foliage.

Once in the car again, he re-lit his cigarette. It was the remains of an earlier one he had planned on finishing later. One he had extinguished back at the shop by crushing its glowing tip between finger and thumb. He exhaled and the car filled with his smoke. It swirled about them, searching for and finally escaping through various gaps in the bodywork. She hated the smell. It took a minute or so but he finally finished. Once again crushing the remains, but this time flicking the butt outside. The blood pounded in her head as she waited. Anticipating his words.

'Let's have a look then,' he said quietly, without even turning in her direction. She knew the drill and went about her business as quickly as was possible in the confines of the car. He moved a bit so she could lie back.

'You know how he used to smirk, Bill? Well I never looked at him. I always shut my eyes. But I could imagine that 'do it or else' look on his face. I can still see it today. It's had a bit of an effect. You know what I mean? I feel really uneasy around older men, even these days.'

'He didn't... I mean he...' Bill found it impossible to say the words, but Kitty guessed his thoughts.

'No. We never did that, if that's what you're thinking. He just enjoyed looking at me. He knew I was completely in his power. If I'd resisted there would have been repercussions. Things were so different back then, weren't they? Kids like us were just, well, obedient I guess. Just did as we were told, like I said before. We didn't have opinions, or the right to speak out. It wasn't our place. Not anything like today you know. If I had, in any way, expressed disapproval, he'd have found some excuse later on to use his belt.'

'Bastard,' Bill muttered. He looked as if he was going to cry, and wished Dwyer was alive today so he could face up to the man and make him answer for his past actions.

While Bill's face showed anger, hers showed relief. It was as if a great weight had been lifted from Kitty's shoulders. This chance to talk openly had been good for her. It had been a long time coming. Bill did not meet Kitty's Frank. Not this time.

'He doesn't and mustn't ever know about Dwyer,' Kitty said in a firm yet hushed tone. I don't want him hurt at all.

'He knows nothing,' she re-emphasised.

'Look, I have to press on,' he said after they had talked some more. 'I'll meet Frank next time, whenever that may be.'

Their reunion was short-lived, but it had been a good one, because they had broken the ice. As she walked him back to his car, Kitty continued to chat but now in a much more relaxed manner than when they had first sat down together. He gave her a brotherly cuddle, and then watched her smiling face in the mirror as he drove off. She waved until he was out of sight.

During the next twenty-four years, Bill caught up with his sister and her lot on dozens of occasions. Kitty and Frank ended up having three children. All boys who took after their dad. A happy, well-adjusted family without a doubt, and when Bill saw his sister in this environment, he knew it was where she deserved to be. Kitty was quick to shout instructions to her youngsters but invariably they did as they wanted, and she went along with it. Typical Kitty, Bill smiled. Say her piece then content to go with the flow. In reality, however, her more casual approach was a deliberate one. Kitty was determined from the outset that her children would have the freedom to express their own thoughts and views, and from an early stage both parents conversed with them as if they were adults and encouraged them to make their own decisions. It was not surprising, therefore, that all three children progressed head and shoulders above their peers at school.

Frank was a gentle type who had no great ambition in life other than to have his own house and raise a family. He and Kitty achieved that goal early in their lives, and as youngish parents, related well to the demands of their growing kids. Their home was of a basic design but in a nice area. It was theirs, and that was the main thing, and as those initial years passed, they felt no great desire to shift to anything better as their friends began doing. Frank liked the idea of becoming debt-free as soon as he could, and that suited Kitty too. She had been through the hardship of low wages after leaving school, and could recall the financial difficulties her parents had experienced when she and Bill had first arrived in New Zealand. Her marriage was successful in many ways, but most of all it was the stability she benefited most from. That more than anything else was something she had craved as a child. That and a loving family.

Early on, Bill helped by ensuring his annual leave was taken to coincide with school holiday breaks. He loved nothing better than to join them each January, when taking a tent and heading for the Pohangina valley just north of Palmerston North was something the kids always demanded. That sort of adventure was the ultimate in enjoyment. Gravel road access, and the rolling Ruahine range lying off to the east. A fortnight's camping on the banks of Coal Creek at a spot known only to a few families. They never knew from one year to another what sort of work he would be doing, for Bill was forever flitting from job to job, place to place. But he would arrive without fail to help them pack, bringing news of his movements over the past months and details of his latest job. He too got comfort from having a stable link to the family, and found himself contributing in the upbringing of the boys by passing on the skills he had gained over many years. They were the new breed. Kids, but 'townie' kids. He showed them how to dam the creek, build a tree hut, and even carve steps and hand-holds up a clay bank. He started things like having a contest for the blackest feet from running barefoot all day, or organising the 'biggest worm' hunt. Simply reinventing things that had come naturally to him and Kitty as children, but which the kids of today ran the risk of missing out on. Times had changed somewhat, and were probably not helped by the arrival of television in New Zealand that same decade.

One visit to their usual camping spot in the late 1960s was fondly remembered, and talked about for years to come as the time they made a boat. An old bathtub secured to the fence by the owner of neighbouring farmland had served his stock well as a makeshift water trough. Bill had other ideas, though, and the three boys helped him drag it down to the creek. Plug-hole bunged shut with a piece of wood to keep it from sinking, their pride and joy was quickly launched with shouts of delight, but was clearly going to be top heavy with anyone in it. It needed some ballast down low, so by quarter-filling with water they eventually had it floating after a fashion, and the boys promptly jumped in while he held it steady for them. Then suddenly they were off, bumping down the first gentle rapid before the current swept their craft out into a deeper pool they had been splashing about in and diving into earlier. The boat rocked dangerously, and they fought hard to keep it upright. Peels of laughter, and the constant shouting of instructions as only boys seem capable of, brought Kitty and Frank to the edge of the creek in time to wave them past. Best holiday ever.

In time the boys got older, pursued other annual interests, and while the letter-writing continued, Bill's visits grew fewer. Eventually the youngsters passed through their teens and began to make their own way in life, with the oldest even planning marriage and talking of his own children to come. Bill was there on the day, proud as ever to be part of the wedding celebration. When the new generation eventually started, Kitty, Frank and their daughter-in-law's parents took an active interest in their grandchildren's upbringing. To differentiate herself, Kitty happily became known as 'Grandma from Palmerston North'.

While Kitty's family had grown and progressed quickly, the years seemed to move at a slower pace for Bill. He continued to keep in touch, telephoning his sister from time to time, and teasing her about being the GM from PN, but more likely using her full title, 'Grandma from Palmerston North'. He told her how comfortable he had become in his new work, having secured a fairly good job in Auckland. Now working for the government, and finding it quite different from anything he had ever experienced before, he had thrown himself into the training and adapted well to the routine.

'And of course they even provide my clothing.'

But later telephone conversations indicated the gloss had faded, although he seemed content enough with it becoming a more sedentary role. The downside was that he put on weight with inactivity, and although Bill had been looking healthier for a long time, his athletic body began turning to fat. Exercise was needed, but he had probably left it too late.

New Zealand climbed slowly into the 1990s and suddenly the turn of the century was within reach. It was the government's idea that each individual made allowance for his or her own future. A long-term personal saving arrangement was the key, and that concept was aggressively promoted for a while. Future governments could not be relied on to provide pensions as they had in the past. Everyone was told this. It was something Bill Wilson was thinking seriously about now. Clearly the country's taxation system would not cope with a future cost of looking after its elderly citizens. Something to do with the changing and reducing ratio of future workers to the number of retired folk. Everyone had an obligation to save for retirement and, until recently, Bill had made no provision for this eventuality. It was his type that current advertising was targeting. Sure his employer had a scheme of sorts, but he had started late in life, so long-term saving had only been a token effort on his part. There was always something on the topic in the *Herald*. People from all walks of life were interviewed, and the furrowed brows of those photographed supported their comments. It seemed the general feeling expressed by 'the man in the street' was that the current government had mismanaged the situation, as had previous governments.

'Opting out,' many said.

'Buy fewer frigates.'

'Stuff the immigrants and refugees'.

'Spend less on supporting those able to, but who won't, work. Bloody dole bludgers.'

Bill recalled how he had opened the paper some time back while on the bus. The photo, one of four interviewees, had been an unmistakable one.

'No,' he had gasped aloud, surprising himself at the venom in his voice at the time, and aware his outburst had drawn glances from other commuters around him. Different name, a foreign one. But the face. That seventy-seven year old face was Dwyer's. No mistake. Bill's blood had almost boiled with the anger of seeing him again.

CHAPTER 13

The old man had done his best to avoid being interviewed that day. There was a big gap until the next group of pedestrians, however, so he had been an easy mark. Although the head down stance and deliberate change of direction showed a distinct lack of interest, his body language was not enough to dissuade the reporter, who stepped forward with confidence. Having arrived in Auckland after many years of drifting, and having gone unnoticed for so long, Dwyer really could not be bothered with the likes of his type, and in any case he preferred to keep to himself. The last thing he wanted was some pushy reporter poking into his business. Manoeuvring the bike that carried his shopping was awkward enough, without being forced closer towards the gutter. The reporter had matched him step for step, and in the end it was easier for the old chap to humour him, rather than making a scene.

'What're after then?' he said with as little enthusiasm in his voice as he could muster.

'Just a few words from you, old fella,' came the reply, as the interviewer selected a fresh page in his notepad. 'Just any comments you want to make about our government's responsibility to look after the elderly.'

'That lot,' he said, referring to the government with contempt. 'Pack of no-hopers aren't they? No, I've nothing to say. Find someone else for your newspaper, mate.'

The reporter picked up on the slight accent in the word 'mate' and took a punt with his next question.

'You're Australian aren't you, sir?'

He had never been addressed as 'sir' before, and while not keen to contribute to the editorial, the old-timer could not help but react.

'Maybe I am, maybe I'm not. But I'll say this to yer, the Aussies look after their pensioners a damn sight better than this lot. They could take a page out of that country's book, if you know what I mean.'

'Thank you very much for that contribution, sir. And your name is?'

'Foulds, now piss off.'

He felt it was the only way to get away, and was not quick enough to manufacture some other fictitious name.

With that last remark, Jim Dwyer shuffled off, leaving the man in the suit scribbling furiously on his pad. He failed to observe the journalist's off-sider with a camera. Weakened eyesight, and the brightness of the day, resulted in his dismissing the flash as being the glint of sunlight off a window or something. Dwyer thought nothing more of the whole incident. And when the article and photograph featured a day or so later, he missed it completely and was none the wiser.

• • • • • • •

It was a 'cock and bull story', and he smiled at how clever he had been to think of it. How he had turned up in casual gear on his day off, and so easily fooled staff members behind the *Herald* counter.

'There, that one. That's mine alright,' Bill said with satisfaction as he leaned over the office counter.

The page with Dwyer's photo lay open between them. He ignored the main character, and pointed to a car parked in the background, confirming it as being his. The one he had had stolen some weeks back, he lied. Helpful newspaper staff let him know the location, and he was shocked to find the photo had been taken outside a butcher's shop not too far from the general area where he himself lived. Another of those coincidences in life.

This was his third visit to the small reserve. If it took months of sitting all day he would do it. He had plenty of accumulated leave, and in any event from time to time needed to get away from his boring job. He could take as long as he liked. Not many butchers in business these days. Most people got their groceries and meat from larger places like Pak'n'Save. Fortunately these older areas of the city still had a number of corner shops worth preserving. Dairies, butchers and the like. It gave an atmosphere of yesteryear about the suburb. It was a feeling about the area that many locals would not want to lose. Years ago people used to hitch their horses to the same railings that remained today outside these small establishments. Bill was one of those who liked the quaintness. The shops had lasted and now, thankfully, developers were unable to pull them down. They were historic places, and gave a sense of stability and permanence that made people want to stay in the area.

It was a long shot. A stab in the dark. No, more a calculated theory. With his employer-related training, Bill was counting on Dwyer having a routine. The photo and text had given the impression of an old guy who was of limited means, not unlike the dero who had stopped for a chat a moment ago. He was sure his quarry lived within walking distance of this very block of shops in front of him, and glanced up and down the road before retreating a safe distance. The weather was settled, and by 9.00 a.m. there were many people coming and going, not wanting to waste time inside. It was going to be another hot day after all. The wind had gone.

In the distance someone was pushing a bike. An old man, making slow, almost painful progress up the hill. Bill watched, having known as soon as he had come into view who it was. The man in the photo plodded towards him. This was definitely Dwyer. The gap between them was closing. Bill wondered how many years since the bike had last been mounted. It seemed these days it was merely something to rest against with a convenient basket hanging off the handlebars. It served its purpose though, and while there were several stops en-route while the man paused to catch his breath, he got there in the end. Propping the bike up against a fence near the mailbox, he shuffled towards the entrance to one of the shops. Bill had already crossed the road in anticipation, and positioned himself in front of a real estate agent's office. He was confident Dwyer would not recognise him, but even so he stood close to the glass, concentrated on the photos in the window, and left plenty of room for the old guy to get past. Bill tensed as Dwyer passed within inches of his back and disappeared inside the shop.

A conversation started almost immediately between the owner and his customer. Louder perhaps than normal for the benefit of an elderly ear. That voice. Unchanged. It made him shiver. And then mid-sentence, a long forgotten phrase from his past.

'Don't you worry, I'll be right in a day or so. Ten bob to a knob of that other stuff, it's just one of those bloody virus things.'

There was only a short delay before Dwyer was in the doorway again.

'See you next week, Mr Foulds, and hope you get over the flu quickly,' came a faceless voice from inside.

Foulds? Same name as mentioned in the newspaper. Not correct though, and Bill found himself on the verge of challenging the error by shouting out DWYER... but something stopped him. An inner voice telling him to wait. He hesitated, decided not to turn, and avoided making eye contact as the man emerged into the sunlight. Accepting it was neither the time nor the place, and that a foolproof plan was required, he concentrated on the window display and let the man pass by. It had to be done properly, first time. Not here while struggling to curb pent-up hatred. With the smell and sound of his abuser so close after all these years it was difficult to remain restrained.

In a rush it all came flooding back. Kitty, his puppy, the fact he thought of Dwyer each morning as he religiously put clothing on in a specific sequence. A silly rule in this day and age, but a habit he had been unable to break. The beatings. The need he had had as a child for a father figure. The fact he and Kitty had been matched up with two great foster parents here in New Zealand, only to be deprived of their love and care so soon afterwards and presented with an alternative in the form of Jim Dwyer. Fun one day, but such an unpredictable ogre the next. And then there was the eventual splitting of brother and sister for much of those precious childhood lives. God, how he hated the man. Hated him with such utter intensity and bitterness.

There would probably only be one opportunity, and it was important to him it had a satisfactory outcome. The last thing he wanted after all this time was to lose the upper hand when it came to a face to face meeting. And there would be a confrontation. Of that he was certain. Bill wanted to see the old bastard squirm, but remained unsure just how far he would go. If Foulds was the name he went by, then the phone book would tell his address and it was probably a safer bet than following him home.

'Please, please let him have a number,' Bill murmured aloud as he headed for a phone box around the corner at a run. Mid-way he hesitated, torn between getting the information and risking losing sight of Dwyer. He had waited too long for this day. Foulds was not listed after all. There were half a dozen entries, but no one living locally. Dashing back to the main road, he watched for a while then decided to let his man slowly disappear into the distance. He would make discreet enquiries in the shop, knowing he had the knack of exacting that sort of information from strangers.

It took hours during the evening to fine-tune his plan of attack but it was that initial step of making contact that worried him most. He promised himself he would, and was determined to do it the following day. The butcher had known Foulds as a regular for many years, and been most forthcoming with information. Even had the address from past Christmas ham order records, and an unlisted telephone number too. It was all Bill needed, and because of its locality, found he was familiar with the street his Mr Martin J Foulds rented a house in. And as luck would have it, he apparently lived alone.

• • • • • • •

'Mr Foulds?'

'Yes... who's that?' came a cautious reply.

It was the questioning voice of someone who did not normally receive inward calls. 'Probably just kept the phone for emergencies,' Bill thought, ignoring the question. It was hard enough speaking to him after all these years, and he was hardly going to give a name immediately. His first priority was to stimulate interest, and the last thing he wanted was for Dwyer to dismiss the conversation as one he could not be bothered with. Having waited so long for him to answer in the first place, he had to be careful with his initial words so Dwyer would not simply hang up. Or worse, sever the call then leave the receiver off the hook for the evening.

'I believe we owe you some money, Mr Foulds.'

The telephone call had come as a surprise. They were few and far between these days, and usually meant confirmation a prescription was ready, the odd call from his one or two friends, or often as not a wrong number. That had not always been the case though. There had been a period some years back, when a party trying to contact the true Martin Foulds had plagued him with calls every other day. Something to do with a relative's loan 'he had guaranteed' and an obligation he had to clear the debt. He had soon put a stop to that harassment by having the telephone service disconnected. He had got used to the idea of not having a phone at all, and when the time came in later years, he successfully arranged an unlisted number to preserve his anonymity.

There was a silence, and the pause gave Bill the impression he had Dwyer's undivided attention. He waited just long enough, then continued before the old man spoke.

'You probably won't remember me. We worked together back in the 1950s. Down south on the Rimutaka tunnel. I'd just started, and I guess you were about to move on.'

Bill paused briefly then continued. He knew Dwyer was listening carefully. He could hear laboured breathing, and felt he had established interest.

'In any event I stayed with the corporation, and now I'm part of their superannuation division.'

Dwyer stammered a bit in the background. No actual words were uttered, but Bill felt the man was thinking. Fidgeting and unsure, but somehow keen to encourage more information.

'My job, well my responsibility really, is to track down employees. You know, those guys we lost contact with. Those guys who should have been receiving pension payments from us for a number of years, but who we have been unable to trace and pay.'

It was time to let him speak. He shut up, and listened to the silence which stretched on and on. Too long perhaps, and Bill contemplated his next words. Until finally, a response.

With what sounded like a great deal of reluctance, Dwyer stammered, 'I... I think you've... um... you've got... you've got the wrong bloke... haven't you, mate?'

'Not at all, Mr Foulds. When I saw your photo, and the article in the newspaper, I recognised you straight away. Mind you, you had me wondering about the name. But we get people changing their names by deed poll for a whole variety of reasons these days. You're lucky I recognised you, Mr Foulds, or should I be calling you, Jim.'

'Photo? Article in the paper? Ah curse them!' Dwyer muttered.

The earlier interview in the street paled into insignificance, however, with the distraction of a potential pay-out.

'How much are we talking about — what did you say your name was?'

'Not a lot, Jim, because you know, you were only there a short time with us. But what with backdating, and all that, let me see. Dwyer, Dwyer... Jim Dwyer, here we are, it's close on $5000 as an up front entitlement, and probably $6.00 per week going forward. It may as well be in your pocket as ours, old fella.'

'I really don't know what to say', said Dwyer not thinking beyond the immediate prospect of some extra money. A tidy amount too, which would not go amiss.

Dwyer had assumed the identity of his hitchhiking friend after retrieving the wallet and other personal effects left in his car for safekeeping. The previous Mr Foulds had had no immediate family, and no one was aware of his demise, so life had carried on. Dwyer had gone bush for many months until things had quietened down. Collecting Foulds' pension years later had posed no problem at all. But it was never enough.

'Can you come in then? Our Auckland office is on the seventeenth floor.'

Bill smiled as he introduced this bit of information in the conversation. He knew it would be inconvenient. All part of his plan.

'Well I...'

'Or perhaps I could bring the papers home for your signature. We could meet this evening if you like. I believe I'm just around the corner from you. Could you come to my home?'

Initially he had hesitated at giving his address. But then, having given the whole matter consideration, he felt more comfortable dealing with him on his own turf.

'Yes that would be easier. So long as you don't mind, that is,' stammered a bewildered Dwyer.

'Excellent,' Bill responded quickly, hoping the keenness to close the conversation off was not too obvious.

'I live in Fir Street. I'll expect you at, say, 7.00 p.m. It's number 20.'

He waited, listening, visualising Dwyer fumbling with pen and paper. He could hear him scribbling the address down. 'Number 20 you say... is that F I R or F U R? Hang on a moment mate, why don't you... how about you come around to my place instead?'

There was a bit of a whine to his voice.

'I'm not too good on my pins these days, and what with it being dark and all...'

'Damn,' Bill thought as he quickly considered this twist in the plan. It was not to his liking. He was losing any advantage he had. Everything had gone so smoothly to this point. He agreed — he had to, and besides he felt it was more important to keep the momentum of their conversation going.

'Yes. Yes. Very well then, I'll see you at 7.00 p.m. But let's make it tomorrow night instead. I've got your address, Jim.'

'Good. See you tomorrow then. Oh, it's the back unit by the way,' Dwyer added hurriedly.

There was no point in saying anything else. Dwyer had already hung up without listening for more.

No harm done, Bill reassured himself as he left his lounge and headed for bed. He would have to rethink things though, and needed to lie down for a while. With Dwyer's agreement to a meeting, an important first step had been taken. He was committed to following through now. But he was still worried, lacking a proper plan. He had yet to carry out a complete and foolproof assessment. And he knew it. A nagging thought plagued Bill that the whole thing might fail, and he had no real idea of how he was going to handle tomorrow's appointment. At least he had an extra day. Initial contact was the biggest hurdle, and that was finally behind him. That was an achievement in itself.

For weeks now Bill Wilson had visualised getting Dwyer in a quiet place, wringing the man's neck with strong hands, and punching his head in with no regard for his own knuckles, before despatching him properly. He thought of the pleasure he would get from wiping a leering smile off his 'uncle's' face. Wiping it off permanently. For once Dwyer would learn about fear and pain. He would be reminded of his past perverted pleasures, and be shown that the day of reckoning had finally arrived. What a shame Kitty's not here, Bill thought. Then again, given the choice, he doubted she would ever want to see Dwyer again. Best she continued in the belief he had died some years back.

Bill found it without too much difficulty. He carried the box of bits and pieces to his bed, having lugged it around from flat to flat over the years. It had been stuffed away in the back of his wardrobe, and contained little-used belongings such as the shanghai his Dad had made out of tyre tube rubber that first week of arrival in New Zealand. A magnifying glass too. He looked at it and cast his mind back, wondering if his initials were still there etched into the veranda boards. Some old birthday cards with loving messages from years ago. No use keeping those now, they could go out. And there it was. His knife. The blades were still in good sharp condition, but opened stiffly. It was some time before his not-so-youthful fingers could move them. Some CRC would soon free those up. The brass rivets in the wooden handle still shone brightly. He hesitated, remembering how he once thought they were made of gold. Used to carry it with him at all times, years ago.

Bill pictured himself in Dwyer's home. He visualised himself yanking the hair back, fully exposing his victim's throat, and cutting through grainy skin. Severing Dwyer's muscles, slicing through tendons, bringing the blade around the back in a long sweep, and working it between the bones until decapitation was complete. The blood would not concern him, for he had gutted the odd animal before and had not been squeamish. Gutted quite a few actually. But could he do the business now? Man to man. And an old man at that. He cast the idea aside. Something to worry about later. Perhaps closer to the time. And then just as suddenly, he dismissed all thought of murdering Jim Dwyer. It was not hard to come to the decision, even though the bastard deserved it. At the end of the day, he had to weigh up the risk, and he rightly decided it was not his place to take the law into his own hands. The authorities needed to be involved here. A belting might be what Dwyer was due. Yes a good hard thrashing with his own belt beforehand. The buckle end, something he would not forget for a long time.

'And it's up to me to administer it,' he said aloud. Then stopped, catching himself before he uttered another word. 'God... I sound just like him.'

CHAPTER 14

It was an easy walk to Dwyer's home. A couple of the streetlights were out, and the partial darkness suited the early evening visitor. A real estate agency sign adorned the wall of the front unit, crying out for offers. 'Quick sale sought'. With a garden needing weeding, and an overall shabbiness, the front property had an absent-owner look about it. A shared access indicated no recent vehicles on its undisturbed, grassed-over driveway. How it would have enhanced both properties had it been concreted. A general tidy-up was needed, and it was of no surprise to him that the place had yet to sell. He walked past the gate, turning back once further up the road. No one else was out and about tonight.

A smell of something rotten ahead of him, when he eventually made his way past an overflowing rubbish bin situated half-way up the path, assailed his nostrils. His first thoughts were that someone should have done something about it, if not for their own well-being, at least to help sell the house in front. The two properties stank, but Foulds, or rather Dwyer's he corrected himself in his mind, was the more presentable of the two. There was a bell, but even so Bill knocked firmly on the door. It seemed more authoritative somehow. The knock of someone in charge.

When he had seen him earlier in the week, for the first time since heaven knows when, he had the impression the old man's eyesight was not the best. He came towards him now. Moving slowly, cautiously. A dark human shape through the glass panel, feeling its way along the wall of a dimly lit passage. A frail old man. The type of person others might possibly take the time to assist if out in the street.

'Are you there?' came the words.

That familiar voice again. So recognisable after all these years. Bill hoped his own voice would not be familiar. No, of course not. Dwyer had only known him as a child.

'Yes, Mr Foulds, I'm here. You do prefer to be known as Foulds, don't you Mr Dwyer?' he asked politely.

It was hard being so courteous, and at the same time saying the hated name aloud, but Bill felt he had to mention the man's correct name to reinforce the fact he had known him in earlier years.

Standing confidently under the porch light, he paid no heed to the moths flicking about his head. He needed to gauge if there was any recognition in this first meeting. There seemed to be none when the door was eventually unlocked and pulled open.

'Come on in then,' said Dwyer ignoring the question and standing aside. A heater had been on for hours it seemed, and Dwyer's flabby gut was visible where buttons on his shirt were either missing or simply left undone. The home smelled warm but stale. Bill's heavy clothing was suddenly inappropriate. He had not counted on it being so much hotter inside, but even so left his coat on. He had no intention staying longer than was necessary.

'Foulds will do,' he finally answered from behind, as he followed Bill on through. That is unless you need me to sign the other name on your papers. You'd better show me what you've got,' he said.

They made their way through to a combination kitchen and living room.

'Take your coat off.'

Bill moved to one side to allow him through. There was still no glimmer of recognition in the eyes. Nothing. Or was there? As he passed he sensed Dwyer squinting. The man stared long and hard.

'Worked with me then did you? Don't remember you at all. Been a long time of course. Late 1950s wasn't it?'

It was Bill's turn not to reply. He stood in the middle of the room and got his bearings.

Dwyer's living room smelled of a recent meal. Sausages probably. It had been cleared away and an uncluttered table awaited them. They sat, and the old man fumbled for something beside him to lean his walking stick against. It slipped, clattered to the floor, and Dwyer cursed. He tried to do something about it, but in the end left it to retrieve afterwards. There was an opened bottle of beer and one glass, which he proceeded to fill. Other bottles were scattered about on the floor. One or two of them broken. While the outside may have been semi-presentable, inside the house it was an utter mess and totally unlike the cleanliness the old man had previously demanded of the kids. Hard to believe his standards had slipped so much.

'Want a coffee, or a beer, or something?'

Dwyer was already settled in his chair. It was a half-hearted offer, which Bill declined.

'No thanks very much, I won't be staying long. Just wanted to get matters sorted.'

Bill kept his coat buttoned and held on to his briefcase. There was no need to open it. Dwyer waited, staring up at the visitor with a look of greedy expectation on his wizened old face. There was an atmosphere of anticipation. But for each man it was for a different reason.

Now or never, Bill told himself. Stop beating about the bush you fool. You've stewed over this for long enough. He looked him squarely in the eye, and raised his voice.

'Yes the 1950s were a long time ago. Actually I haven't brought any papers with me, you dirty old prick. And I'm not the person I said I was on the phone.'

There it was. A blurted-out statement, loud and clear. And one which marked the passing of a point of no return. Dwyer's expression changed. He was unable to fathom the reason for this sudden loud outburst. There was a look of disbelief, and complete confusion on his face.

'What's going on? What do you mean? Who the hell are you anyway?' he whined.

Then it happened. Bill was waiting for it, and he caught that initial, faint sign of recognition. He watched as Dwyer dismissed it. But then it grew again, and the old man's eyes narrowed as he reluctantly accepted the fact.

Dwyer had taken a long time to get over the fact that he, the hunter, had failed to capture two miserable kids in the bush. It had been a real slap in the face for him at the time. The years had diminished the memory, but today salt was being well and truly rubbed into an old wound. Now one of them had successfully tracked and caught him. He sensed this man sitting before him was here to right a wrong. A reversal of sorts. A new hunter and a new quarry. Yes, he had been tracked and trapped. There was little he could do but lean back and sneer.

'So what's your game then, Bill?'

'So you remember me do you? Kitty and me. The floggings?'

'Oh, I remember all right. Little brats.'

'Perhaps we both tested you at times, Dwyer, but what you did to us, and tried to do to my sister... well I guess you know I'm aware of what went on.'

'That little red-headed slut,' he sneered, 'what's she been saying?'

The derogatory reference to his sister was all that was required. Enough had been said in this short space of time, and Bill now had his excuse to act. Lurching forward, he pushed the table towards the old man. Earlier he had fondled the reassuring shape of the instrument in his pocket. Felt that familiar metal skull on the bone handle. But now in the rush of activity, there was no time for a knife, not even to threaten him with. Dwyer began to rise. He was not quick enough, and his unsteadiness was a distinct disadvantage. Half-turning he staggered, then fell back heavily, tripping on the walking stick, crashing amongst bottles and glasses. Bill leapt forward, taking advantage of his superior position. A good hard punch was what was needed now, to get things moving. But the opportunity to deliver a blow or two did not eventuate, and the likelihood of his laying into him with the hard end of a belt suddenly seemed even more remote.

Dwyer lay moaning and writhing, making no attempt to protect himself. He cared not that he might be attacked. He had a bigger problem to deal with. Bill had yet to touch the man, but it was clear he was severely injured. The broken bottles and shattered beer glasses. That fat white belly of his. A horrendous gash in the flesh. Blood pumping freely. These were the things Bill saw as the whole scene swirled around him. A large piece of something protruded from the wound. The old man was in a very bad way. Bill paused, taking it all in, watching as Dwyer clasped his hand over the spot, struggled to stem the flow and tried to stand. His hands, wet with blood, hampered his efforts and he was having difficulty seeing how badly damaged he really was. Everything was slippery. Beer and blood. There was no way he was going to get up from his knees.

'Help me, damn you. Help me!'

It was not that Bill was squeamish or that he could not help. Hell, for a brief time he had killed animals for a living, he thought to himself. It was just that there and then he made a conscious decision that he would not assist the man. Dwyer sensed it. He leaned back against the wall, realising the only one able to offer help would be making no effort to assist him at all. He looked at Bill with utter contempt.

'I'm an old man, and I need help, bugger you. Give me that phone.'

Bill picked it up, and deliberately held it out of reach. He stepped back from the mess. It had been years since he had seen so much blood. Nothing was said. Dwyer lay there whimpering like a whipped dog. Unable to move, and not knowing what to do or what to expect. Bill watched him cautiously, knowing Dwyer's type often gathered strength in one last superhuman effort. The old man raised his head, and looked at his attacker again, but the strain on his face showed he was sinking fast. Bill recognised the signs. The pale sweating skin. The short gasping breath.

Dwyer lay down flat on the floor trying as best he could not to disturb the wound. He needed to conserve what little energy he had left. The weight of his body pushed the gash against the floorboards, causing him to cry out in pain. He needed the weight of his body to help stop the flow of blood.

Bill felt nothing for him, but asked the question anyway. 'How does it feel to really hurt?'

He hoped Dwyer was feeling as sick as possible.

'Think of what you put the two of us through, you bastard. Especially Kitty.'

Dwyer said nothing. His breathing was shallow, and he had stopped the shivering and twitching that had been evident earlier when shock first set in. Bill waited another forty minutes. There had been no further movement. Not even when he nudged him hard with his foot, partially rolling the victim onto his back. No reaction, no sound either. Eyes closed, gash still weeping. While the wound appeared to have almost closed, it was nevertheless extremely large. Perhaps large enough to take a whole fist if someone had felt inclined to stem the flow. It was time he left.

Bill Wilson checked carefully. There was nothing to show he had been there. No empty cup to indicate a visitor's acceptance of a drink. Nothing left behind. He had not even put down his briefcase. He stood, ripped the top page off a pad on the table where Dwyer has scrawled his address during the previous evening's telephone conversation, and walked backwards out of the room. The door shut easily with a flick of his foot. Hadn't touched a thing. Yes, he had. The phone. He crept back silently now, as if not wanting to wake the man. With receiver wiped clean, he cradled it in Dwyer's own hand so as to get the owner's bloody prints onto it. The body lay almost lifeless and well beyond help. But yanking the telephone cord from the wall was a final safeguard, just for good measure, he told himself before leaving.

No one in the front unit. No car to start. It was dark. All these were positives. He left the door open, allowing warmth to drain from the house. Why leave any last comforts? There was a chill in the outside air. Within minutes Bill was down the road and nearing his own home. His keys were caught up with his knife when he pulled the tangle from his pocket. 'Not needed after all,' he thought thankfully.

Have I been out at all tonight? he asked himself with a smile of satisfaction. 'Not me.'

• • • • • • •

Local police stations could easily be operated as sole charge affairs these days. They were more an outpost where you reported lost property and the like, without the hassle of a journey into 'Central'. This one's cell out back had not housed an occupant for ages, and for the past few years had been used strictly for storage. The general condition of the building even reflected the status it held these days within the police force. Another quiet day in the suburb.

'So how long have you been permanently based here?' asked today's relief from Central.

'Too long,' came the reply.

The senior constable was not one for conversation. He was unlikely to even admit an appreciation for a colleague's company. In fact, most felt he took exception to their presence. But there it was. Policy stated no less than two officers, and so the sole charge role he had enjoyed in recent years had become a thing of the past. Three relatively new recruits had been taking it turn about to provide the second officer relief. It was easy duty for them for a day or so before boredom crept in. Their weekly assignments could not finish soon enough.

Senior, or 'Tucker' as he was affectionately known, listened to their accounts of the faster pace elsewhere. He had seen a bit of it. Done his time. But a return to a more active role held no appeal for him these days. He had been there, and he often told them so. 'Tucker' enjoyed his sleepy corner of the world. This tired part of Auckland where little out of the ordinary ever occurred suited him just fine. The jobs he enjoyed most included stakeouts. Those assignments where he simply had to wait, and manually record the comings and goings of suspects and others. Usually car conversion gangs, warehouse raids they had been tipped off about, even the activities of unfaithful partners. Laziness on his part? Even 'Tucker' had no idea. He felt it was a time in his life when he deserved the odd no-brainer job. Such activities gave him just enough satisfaction, a continued income, and were sufficient to stave off complete boredom. Really it was just one pointless job replaced by another one when you got down to it, but 'Tucker' never complained. He got something out of his waiting and watching roles.

The overweight policeman excused himself and ambled outside into sunlight. Small windows in a building like theirs afforded limited natural daylight within. 'Tucker' shielded his eyes against the brightness, having decided it was time for another smoke or something to eat. Or both. The time dragged, but seemed not to affect him the way it did his colleagues. Probably because he was used to it. Probably because he had been brought up with no real ambition or goals in life. For many years he had been content to simply coast along, having joined the force later than others, and having always felt somewhat disadvantaged by this fact. As a result he had been offered, and gladly accepted, this current position. With no family commitments it was a basic but comfortable life. He enjoyed the authority he had and he enjoyed his food. Hence the nickname 'Tucker'. New recruits, like this one today, were simply asked to report to 'Tucker'.

'Tea's up,' came the voice from inside.

'About time too,' he replied with renewed enthusiasm, as his fag butt was expertly flicked out into the street. 'I'll have my bread roll with that brew.'

• • • • • • •

Dwyer's head lifted slightly and he listened for any sound of his intruder. At some stage he had managed to get back on to his stomach with the weight of his body providing the much-needed pressure to keep his gash closed. But now he found he could hardly move. He tried, but the attempt brought forth a surge of pain, and even in his weakened state he realised he was unlikely to make it through to the morning. But at least he was alone.

'Bastard,' he hissed, wondering as he said the word through clenched teeth whether it would be the last he ever uttered. He lay quietly in the pool of sticky blood. His mind was working. Scheming as ever. He moved his hand slowly away from the wound. The blood had congealed. But what covered his fingers was still wet, and sufficient for him to leave a message. He would write his attacker's name... in blood. But what name? He knew him as Bill Wilson, but after being placed in welfare care had the boy been adopted? What surname did he go under these days? Dwyer was too weak to think. He gave up, slipping back into a state of semi-consciousness for a while. His body needed further rest. It was only for a moment though. A small skerrick of information plagued him. His head swam, and that distant thought began to crystallise. His fuddled mind started to clear, enough for him to remember. The address. He knew his attacker's address. Bill lived at 20 Fir Street. With a blood-caked finger, Dwyer began to trace the letters.

Painfully. Slowly. He was delirious, and his mind failed to take the easiest route. He did not think to simply print the numbers. As each finger dried he swapped it for another. In bold print he wrote **T W E N T Y** and then rested. Under that, the letters of the street **F I R.** With difficulty, but with great satisfaction, he finished the abbreviation for street with a clearly defined full stop. Dwyer slumped forward. Tired, sore, intending to rest, but only briefly. His head cleared for a moment, and he thought of how he would get up later on. How he would leave Auckland, and go down-country to where he had lived years ago. Some place where he could lose himself again in a rural community. One of his old haunts. They were unlikely to remember him. It would be good to go back. It would take time, but he could do it. These were the thoughts that coursed though his mind, and gave him a temporary focus as he lay trying desperately to regain some strength. Things seemed to be turning dark. His eyes closed.

• • • • • • •

'What do you make of that?' the constable asked, pointing out the wording to 'Tucker'.

They had pulled back the tatty living room curtains, and the scene was clearer now in the natural light.

'Written in blood, eh,' he continued, stepping cautiously amongst broken glass while the senior officer stood back and stared long and hard at the message scrawled on dirty floorboards and listened to his younger colleague's comments.

A concerned real estate agent who had become more aware as the days passed of an open door and general lack of activity, had alerted them to the house.

'I'd say there'll be a body around here somewhere,' Tucker contributed at last. 'Colour of that blood indicates this all happened about eight or ten days ago. It's the thirtieth today, so that would make it about the twenty-first.'

'T W E N T Y F I R S T,' said Tucker slowly, linking the smeared letters together.

'Looks like he was trying to tell us the date of his accident,' he explained to the new recruit, emphasising the point.

'Or his murder. Poor bugger.'

Tucker dismissed his offsider's comment, explaining it was unlikely anyone else was involved. 'Doubt it. Lived on his own, and had nothing anyone would have wanted. Bit of a hermit as I understand. Kept to himself by all accounts. No, I reckon he must have tripped on his stick and fallen on the bottles. Seems to have busted the phone trying to raise someone,' suggested Tucker. Yes, I think that's a pretty fair summary. Did it himself.'

The recruit agreed.

'You'd better follow the usual procedure. The others will be here soon. But I'd say that's a logical explanation, wouldn't you? I dare say they'll come to the same conclusion. Write your assumption in your report, young fella. I'll confirm it. You never know, it may help convince the bloody detectives if they're a little undecided.'

They checked the other rooms, then Tucker stepped outside where the air was cleaner. With steady hands cupped around his cigarette, he struck a match and flicked it well clear of the investigation area. Strolling slowly down the driveway he searched for clues. There was no obvious smell of a corpse, but then the offensive aroma from a rubbish bin between the units would likely disguise that anyway. Having joined the force later when they needed people to man these quieter areas, he had missed career opportunities, and watched as younger ones progressed. Leadership responsibilities did not appeal, and he had not been trained as an investigating officer. He had never wanted to be a detective, but he knew what to look for. There was too much blood inside. He expected to find a body. It would not surprise him if they found the occupant lying dead not too far from the house. He paid particular attention to shrubbery and the hedging hiding a neighbouring property from view. He strolled along as if expecting to find where the victim had crawled into foliage to hide. He walked slowly and looked carefully. Searching out the nooks and crannies, as if he knew his man. He would be here somewhere. They would find him eventually. Perhaps later in the day.

Tucker walked slowly down the driveway with hands rummaging about in the depths of his uniform pockets. His fingers closing around the handle of a knife he had had almost all his life. His thumb gently caressed the smooth brass rivets, and traced the familiar shape of the skull. He smiled a deeply satisfying smile. Bill 'Tucker' Wilson thought of his sister Kitty, and for the first time in many years, of his dog Trix.

An investigation can so often be a laborious process, but the end result is often worth the wait. Not on this occasion, however. In this particular case, the little information available dictated an early culmination to the enquiry. After only three weeks of semi-intensive work, and with no family members pushing for ongoing action on the part of the police, the file covering the suspicious absence of a known tenant from a blood-spattered Auckland rental property was cast aside. One file that could be placed in the non-urgent tray meantime, but also one that might never again be referred to.

Senior constable Bill Wilson was not satisfied with progress, but it was a matter that was out of his hands. Of course he had a vested interest in the case, having been personally involved on the night of the incident. But that fact could never be revealed. Although not the most career-minded of officers, he was fed up with the low success rate they had at times, and the fact these were caused, more often than not, by staffing shortages within the force. In his spare hours he returned to the scene, searching fruitlessly for any clue that may have gone unnoticed. Cautiously making enquiries and checking nearby parks and reserves for the decomposing body he was convinced lay somewhere close by. Making sure when speaking to anyone, that he substituted 'Foulds' as the name of the potential victim rather than the name that came most readily to his lips. In the end he resigned himself to the fact that, somehow, miraculously, the old man had survived. Given his age and injury, Dwyer's regained strength amazed him. But then again, somehow it did not. Dwyer had always been a cunning bugger, and it was obvious now that he had not been as severely hurt as he had made out.

It had been more than a month, and despite the ongoing staffing shortages, Bill 'Tucker' Wilson was once again under pressure to get rid of accumulated leave on a 'use it or lose it' basis. He had five weeks to take, and in the end accepted the reasoning behind it all. Finally made sense of the fact that he needed to get away from his job, and it was while contemplating a forced break from duty and the hussle and bustle of the city that a strange thought dawned on him. It was a long shot but he would give it further consideration that evening. His period of leave commenced this Friday, and in the meantime there was a pile of paperwork to get behind him. He needed to concentrate on the job at hand. He was pleased he had an inside job today, with the sound of drizzle on the roof indicating more wet weather to come. There would be time to think of Dwyer later on.

CHAPTER 15

Thankfully, as the month ended, improved weather the experts had forecast eventuated. A portion of line just south of Pukekohe restricted rail traffic to a slow pace as track conditions forced a reduction in speed. And then, despite their immense power, the slight gradient that followed made diesel locomotives struggle for a while before regaining that lost momentum. It was an ideal spot to hitch a free ride.

Dwyer sat patiently in the dark. It had been a pleasant enough day, but now the sun had gone down the grass had become wet with night moisture and he was starting to feel cramp in his elderly legs, and general discomfort. Crouching there on the lupin-covered embankment, he watched as an approaching train's massive headlight lit up the cutting. He sat unseen as the beam illuminated everything about him but also created shadows. Dwyer was used to lurking in shadows and waited his chance. Notwithstanding his age and recent injury, when the moment came he would move with agility. He needed to because it was unlikely he would get another opportunity this evening. The engine noise increased, as it stormed ahead much faster than he expected. Carriages trundled by, some lit up, others in darkness, each with its own squeaks and rattles. Individual noises caused by metal on metal.

It took him a bit by surprise when the last one rounded the bend. A much shorter train this evening, not the lengthy one he had envisaged. Despite many years on the tracks with New Zealand Rail gangs, he was now clearly out of touch with freight movement. Dwyer gathered his coat and few belongings, and set off down the slope, selecting one of the last carriages as he ran. A darkened one that appeared to be empty. No point in having an audience. In a few arthritic strides he had positioned himself close to the rails, and while still moving forward looked back at the advancing steps and handrail. The stones underfoot unnerved him a bit, but using a tried and true technique he heaved himself up, slipping at the end and sprawling awkwardly and heavily on the metal floor. The old man stayed where he was in that space between carriages, content to just sway with the motion of the train, and quietly thanking those who had helped his recovery. Without them there would have been no way he could have jumped this train. Gasping loudly, he lay watching the sleepers flash past in a blur beneath him. Listening to the rhythmic sound the wheels made as they came in contact with joints in the track. Not his best performance tonight, but good enough, and anyone looking at the expression on his unshaven face could only have described it as one of pure satisfaction. It had been a supreme effort. With heart racing, and body perspiring, the cool breeze was welcome relief as the train increased its pace.

Dwyer waited longer than was probably necessary listening for the dreaded sound of footsteps. Giving anyone aboard who had witnessed his arrival the chance to challenge him. It did not happen, and with wheels settling into a steady rhythm, the trip through Meremere and the backwaters of Te Kauwhata passed quickly. He eventually rose, entered the empty carriage, and made himself at home knowing he could do with an uninterrupted sleep. By early next morning they would be passing through Palmerston North, and it would suit him best if they carried on through the gorge to the Wairarapa rather than straight down the west coast of the island towards Wellington.

His injury still hurt and he felt fragile. It had not been the most sensible method of boarding a train, but he felt it the best way to leave Auckland. Dwyer was mindful of security cameras and the possibility, in some situations, of having to present identification. He simply wanted to get to his destination with the minimum of fuss, and besides a long-established hunting instinct had driven him once again to moving from point to point without trace. Thoughts returned to the Salvation Army staff who had been kind to him. They had cared for him these past weeks in one of their hostels for the homeless, assuming he was just another old chap who had got himself caught up in a fight. He had heard them talking about it when thinking he was asleep. They had had their difficulties with him initially, when he steadfastly refused treatment. But as the days passed, and when the pain eventually proved too much, Dwyer had gratefully accepted a few pills, and those had knocked him out for a while. There were no complaints from him the following day when he found he had been attended to. He felt better for the clean dressings, and those antibiotics had knocked his flu' on the head too. The opportunity to stitch his wound had long passed, and he had been lucky the gash had started to knit together naturally. It had been a bit rotten, they had informed him. The nurse had caught it just in time. Sure it still smelt a bit, but then so did he, as did others in the temporary beds around him. Of course the wound had been worse on the night of the confrontation. A pretty bad cut, but he had managed to stem the flow simply by lying still for so long. Patience on his part had enabled the blood to congeal. He was told the wound would leave a permanent and vividly raised scar, but Dwyer had known from his pig sticking days that although taken by surprise it never ever had the makings of a mortal cut. 'Needed to be far deeper than that to take me out,' he had thought to himself during his convalescence.

Having been patched up and properly fed, Dwyer regained his strength and was soon thinking of his next move. He was forever planning, to ensure he kept one step ahead of the authorities. With recent events foremost in his mind, he decided it would be safer to hunt out one of his old haunts from the 1950s. A fresh start was required, somewhere far from Auckland. Somewhere familiar to him, but not where he would be remembered. The boy's arrival on the scene after all this time had made him think long and hard about those earlier years. It was unlikely he would be recognised where he was heading. Unlikely anyone from his past in the Wairarapa was still even resident in that area. Nevertheless he would get there, and check it out discreetly in a few days' time. He had to be more careful from now on.

Dwyer was fearful of the consequences if the boy caught up with him again, and certainly did not want the cops involved. He had no idea at all that Bill was himself a policeman. Looking back he realised he had a lot to answer for, and they would have enough to make it stick if ever they set their minds to it. Not just here in New Zealand either.

• • • • • • •

Bill packed his gear in two soft bags and stowed them in the corner of his room. Just his toothbrush and a flannel required to complete matters in the morning, and then he would be off. He loathed early deadlines, but the bus left at the crack of dawn and that was that. He would get a taxi to the terminus at 'stupid o'clock'. Bill smiled as he remembered that phrase from his childhood. Something Kitty used to say. The smile lingered only briefly. He had been annoyed to find his car had started slipping out of gear again, and it had been an easy decision not to chance it on the long trip south. He felt his pocket again, reassuring himself he still had the ticket. That was the thing about New Zealand. A small country like this meant you could get from one end to the other in a matter of days. Hours if you were prepared to fly.

He considered his reasoning once more. Resurrected the idea that had come to him. Tried to think as Dwyer would have thought. It was a wild plan but his options were limited. If he had been Dwyer, he would have wanted to get out of Auckland to some place where he could just slip back quietly into the community. Of course Dwyer had survived for decades, and could have had a multitude of preferred places to choose from. This was the unknown factor Bill had hanging over him, but he had to ignore it. Even if Dwyer was not heading back to the Wairarapa, this whole sequence of events over past months had resulted in the resurrection of unpleasant memories, and a visit to that house just out of Greytown was not going to do any more damage than had already been caused. In fact, it just might be the thing to bring closure to a chapter of his life that had been affecting him for too long. It was worth a try, and besides he could not escape from this burning gut feeling that he and Jim Dwyer were on the same path and would meet again in that isolated cottage. If in fact it still existed.

Right there and then he cemented in his mind that he would catch the old bastard. He was confident Dwyer could not give him the slip a second time, and what better outcome than to track him back to the scene where it had all started those many years ago. He was more determined than ever now to finish the task. Why had he become so confidant Jim Dwyer would head for that particular destination? This was a thought that nagged at him as he considered the facts, and following a tried and true procedure of weighing up pros and cons using his policeman's questioning mind. Or was it simply a process developed in those formative years, when the basis of Bill Wilson's thinking was influenced by the man he now pursued. The hunter in him was emerging, working in harmony with the mind of a cop. And he thought the expression 'cop' was appropriate today because Dwyer was going to cop it all right. He was sick of graffiti everywhere, the insolence of the youth of today, the court system that regularly let the force down, and those who flouted the law. Despite a normally rational mind, it was time he did in fact take matters into his own hands.

Had he been able to get work-related affairs in order more quickly, Bill would have caught the late train. It had left hours earlier, however, and he settled for the early morning's bus rather than waiting a further day. The trip would be just as comfortable. Erosion had apparently resulted in a derailment some kilometres beyond Taumaranui during the week. He had heard of this in advance, and knew it would slow up the rail trip anyway. When booking his seat by telephone, the ticketing girl had been helpful with options available to him.

'There's every likelihood your bus will connect with the train at Palmerston North during the afternoon anyway. They're going to have a very long trip on that one unfortunately.'

• • • • • • •

Dwyer's sleep was disturbed a number of times during the night when they had had to stop. He felt ill at ease when the bright lights of a station platform intruded into his carriage. On one occasion he had vacated the carriage, and been forced to wait quietly on the far side of the train while activities in the station took place. Too many people about for his liking. He could not understand the four hour delay at Te Kuiti, and longed for a decent hot cuppa to warm his insides. At last they completed the addition of a couple of freight wagons, and he decided to seek refuge in one of them for the remainder of his journey. He did his trick of jumping aboard as they moved out of the siding, and settling down with no further thought of the likelihood of detection. The train stopped for a similar period at Taumaranui, but Dwyer slept through this one. He was annoyed, therefore, when he awoke later to find it creeping along at a snail's pace past the type of railway gang he had spent many years working with. All leaning on their shovels just as he had done in his younger days. The work required to fix the track damage was extensive, and accounted for the reason they were so far behind time. He thought they would be earning a bit on this job, looking at the team working under lights. He glanced at his watch and scowled, expecting to be a couple of hundred kilometres further south of this point by now.

'Nothing I can do about it I suppose,' he muttered out loud to the wagon's emptiness. 'Not going to bloody walk.'

Dwyer sat with legs dangling over the side, and watched the workers' faces peering up at him. His train was moving, but only just. And then soon enough the gang was left behind. He knew the country well, this side of Taumaranui down through the national park, by-passing Raetahi. He had spent a couple of seasons on the carrot farms in the area and had made good money. That was a while back now. Ohakune came and went in a flash and soon they were passing Tangiwai, the very place the kids' parents had perished back in the 1950s in a separate accident to the well-known rail disaster. Dwyer gave it no thought at all, even when they did the traditional slowed pace at the bridge site. The train increased speed once beyond the isolated spot, flashing past hillocks of sub-alpine snowgrass in this area of high altitude desert. Only another corner or two and the snowy image of Ruapehu in morning light, cut in half today by a ring of low cloud, would be lost forever behind the foothills. He willed the train on, looking forward to the faster stretches of track that lay ahead as they raced down from the central plateau. At this pace it would not take them long to make up some of the lost time. He was wrong. The earlier delay now meant a further wait of almost three hours at Taihape in order to let those using the lines in a northerly direction to continue to remain on schedule. It was a discontented and utterly frustrated Jim Dwyer who lay back in an otherwise empty wagon and slept the afternoon away.

A gentle pull into Palmerston North caused a change in the 'click-clicks' from the rails, and this irregularity eventually aroused him from his slumber. They were back to a walking pace, enabling Dwyer to swing once more to the ground so he could do the last 300 metres on his own. It was as if he had never been aboard. Simply some old chap taking a shortcut across the railyards, or at least that was the impression he wanted to give. Only a few travellers and rail staff on the platform, but there was yet another wait while a busload of new passengers from Auckland hurried to find spare seats in the front carriages. They had come a more straightforward route down the desert road, in the hope of connecting before the train changed direction and headed through a gorge to the Wairarapa.

• • • • • • •

Bill Wilson had enjoyed the ride, seeing a different view from the bus's raised seating. The North Island's central desert had a raw natural beauty he had missed in the past when having to concentrate on driving. Erosion caused by extremes of climate and abrasive winds was evident, but it was easy to look past all this at the majesty of the terrain. From way up high snow-melt trickled, then flowed, through deeply incised cuttings before joining as one body of water. The sun had been sparkling on that distant flowing mass when they passed by today, and his thoughts were on the river that had taken his parents. Bill had stared in silence, reflecting on the gentle couple he had known for too short a period and, who at the time of their deaths, had just reached the best part of their lives.

Dwyer used the station's public toilets, then made his way along a tar-sealed platform, slowly passing windows filled with bored and tired commuters. Bill Wilson, engrossed in his magazine, was oblivious to the comings and goings of people on the other side of the glass. Similarly Dwyer, head bowed and with a shuffling gait, passed the window completely unaware of the fact he would be sharing a train to the same destination as the man who was hunting him. Five thirty on the dot, and they were on the move again. Somehow Dwyer had managed to get a seat in a rear carriage this time, without having to produce a ticket. He was pleased to be inside on more comfortable seating where it would be warmer, and his forward facing seat ensured he had plenty of warning if the guard returned. A draughty freight wagon was not the most ideal means of transport in the chill of an evening.

For those continuing through to Wellington there was a trip of three hours ahead of them. Bill checked his watch, knowing he would be disembarking in just over an hour at Masterton. With a room booked at one of the local hotels, he looked forward to a steaming hot bath and a good night's sleep. Rental car arrangements he had intended making that evening could be finalised in the morning now. If the old house was still there, he planned to park well beyond it and sneak back. Cross-country if need be. He would not rush things, and assumed he would still recognise the place. Remembering his initials on the veranda boards, he struggled but could not recall whether he had burned them there using a magnifying glass, as he thought he had, or actually carved them with the knife he still carried.

The train backtracked in an easterly direction towards Ashhurst before rumbling slowly across the Manawatu river rail bridge, then hugged the northern side as it continued on through the gorge. The ride in a southerly direction again would begin at Woodville, and from that point on commuters would glimpse the rising land to their right as the Tararua range grew in size. The light of the day was quickly fading, but it was enough for Bill to see the Wairarapa valley had not been affected by urban sprawl as had places like Auckland. It had been a long time since he had ventured this far south. The view from the carriage window was an unchanged one, almost like going back in time.

With smaller towns delaying them only briefly, speed was increased through the Eketahuna stretch, and soon street lights heralded Masterton's outskirts. In next to no time he found himself manhandling bags into a taxi and giving instructions to the driver. The short rail portion of his trip had flashed past and for that he was thankful. Overall it had been a long and tiring day.

'You've got good weather forecast for the next week or so. If you're wanting some sightseeing in the area, only too pleased to oblige.'

'No thanks, they've got a rental booked for me. Just want to check out the area. It's been a few years since I was last here. I'll probably take the car on to Wellington, and fly back to Auckland after my visit.'

The driver scoffed at the mention of Auckland, but it was a lighthearted reaction. He had never been there himself, but had heard enough from others.

'This is it then, is it?'

'Yep, one of the older ones, but very good meals they tell me.'

Bill paid the required amount, and with a bag in each hand pushed his way through the heavy swing doors to be greeted by the usual smell associated with an old hotel.

• • • • • • •

Dwyer thought twice about leaving the warmth of his seat, but in the end elected to get off at either of the next two towns. Carterton or Greytown, it mattered not. They were virtually the same distance from where he was heading, and it would not be too late for a local dairy to fix him up with the items of food he was after. Tinned stuff, couple of spuds, something good and sharp to peel them with. Once that was organised, he would set off on foot towards the ranges. There would be a barn or some such he could use for the night. Hell, he would even consider a bobby calf cage at a farm gate where they put animals ready for the works if it came to that.

Despite his age, the long walk ahead of him was something he was looking forward to. He had been sitting too long, and relished the idea of putting some distance between himself and civilisation. And if there was any traffic on the back road he could simply step off into the undergrowth and wait for it to pass. No one would have any idea he was in the area. The old man settled back in the empty carriage listening to the familiar 'click-clunk', 'click-clunk' as its wheels hit expansion gaps in the rails, eventually falling into a quieter pattern once the train got up to speed again. He dozed for a while, but with no great distance between towns it was not long before a change in the sound of the rails told him they were slowing again. For a brief moment he wondered whether it would be wiser to forget his plans, and carry on through the Rimutaka tunnel to search out one of many disused NZR huts he had once known about on the Trentham side. But with no way of telling whether natural progress had resulted in the demolition of those rail houses, it was only a wild thought. At least this side of the range had been virtually unaffected by population growth, unlike Auckland's sprawl. Wellington was probably the same as Auckland, he decided. As his carriage slowed to a walking pace, Dwyer readied himself by gripping the handrail, and hanging out from the step with one leg swinging free. He remained uncertain right up until the last possible moment, unsure whether to let go or pull himself back into the warmth. In the end he made his decision, and with the agility of someone far younger in years, and with the whole night ahead of him, Dwyer set off to find a dairy for supplies and a knife and then to continue his journey towards the distant foothills.

Beyond him, and dwarfing everything below it, was the shapeless bulk of the range. He had set foot on almost every square metre of land up there. Hundreds of times with a rifle and once chasing those brats. Rising high above the undulating land ahead of him, its ridges and peaks were illuminated by eerie moonlight in a way that was vaguely familiar. It was an ominous scene reminiscent of a time he had spent in a national park just south of Melbourne, before coming to New Zealand. That was a while back too, but for just a brief moment the soft light brought back those memories and Dwyer felt hesitant and slightly vulnerable.

CHAPTER 16

Summer had certainly returned to the Wairarapa, judging by the dry grass either side of the highway. It spread out forming a sunburned carpet of farmland. Sheep huddled together in any bit of shade they could find, and this year the air seemed almost too hot to breathe. The whole countryside shimmered in the heat of the day.

A young couple and their children drove up one of the winding roads that linked State Highway 2 with the Tararua foothills. Venturing east from Wellington, then up in a northerly direction, they had the full day ahead of them to explore new territory. During previous months, coastal and rural properties on the western side of the range had been checked and dismissed, and they were beginning to fear they would never find exactly what it was they had in mind. Like many, it was their dream for a place within an hour or so from home, but far enough away to effectively escape from the city for weekends. Their enthusiasm for having a holiday home had been widely discussed with extended family, although there had been a recommendation, almost an insistence from that quarter, they restrict their search to the sunny western coast above Wellington if they were going to look at all. Perhaps somewhere nice and handy for friends and family to visit. In the end they had to ignore that preference, heading instead for the more distant Wairarapa area.

They had seen a number of places today, all described by the real estate agents as being pre-loved rural homes. Pretty run down, most of them. Armed with a map and instructions, they continued to assess and discount potential addresses as they worked their way further from the main highway. The family of five eventually found themselves following a Masterton agent's instructions that took them into a small sheltered valley linked to the local town by a recently sealed road. Late in the afternoon they came across a farm cottage that was one of the last on their list. It was still pretty sound, but the grounds had not been tended for many years. All in all they were pleasantly surprised at their find.

• • • • • • •

Earlier in the day, Dwyer had stepped off the road about a kilometre from the house, and pushed though a thin patch of blackberry to get out of sight. On reaching the paddock he followed the direction of the road, content to be walking in soft wet grass. He had put in the miles, but had also rested up for many hours before breakfasting on his meager food supply and then pressing on again. The sun was up, but in the shade of the hedge he knew he was invisible to anyone in passing vehicles and while there had been little traffic anyway, he was happier approaching the house in this manner. He remained convinced it would be empty, but if not he had other plans in mind for his long-term accommodation.

The surrounding terrain and paddocks had remained virtually unchanged. In some places it was just as he remembered it. Even fencing seemed not to have been replaced. They had lasted well, and he thought of how he used to climb the wires to set off over this same ground when making for the bush for an evening's shoot. It was at a much slower pace that he moved these days, needing frequent stops for rest as the ground rose steeply to a high point. Finally he could sit for a while and look down on the valley. The original trig station had long gone. Now a steel marker set in concrete was the lonely guard of these hills. Many initials were scratched in the paintwork, much like the mild vandalism on the old wooden tripod that had stood before.

Below him he could see the house in a sorry state of disrepair. It looked different somehow. Not so hemmed in as it used to be, but certainly a good place for a squatter. Yet at the same time he was uneasy. A sixth sense told him all was not quite right. Torn between waiting, yet keen to get off the hill and inside, he hastily and perhaps carelessly convinced himself he was alone in the area and picked his way as quickly as he could down the uneven slope. No one saw him approaching. The home had not been occupied for several years and was still out of sight from neighbouring properties.

• • • • • • •

From the long driveway the surrounding trees provided welcome shade. There had been bigger ones years ago, but they must have really crowded the house. At some stage a keen person had had the foresight to remove the largest ones, and now the only evidence they had ever existed was in the large weathered marcrocarpa stumps rising like well-spaced tomb stones from the grass.

Approaching the house, the two adults and three children drank in the scene, noting boards missing from veranda and porch.

'Easily fixed,' the man announced with confidence as the group picked their way carefully along what seemed to be the soundest portions of the veranda structure. It needed a lot of work and the family trod cautiously. In part it was as much a fear of falling through, as it was the probability of disturbing someone in residence. That was hardly likely though. According to their notes it was unoccupied.

'It's a shame really. Place seems in pretty good overall condition. Look, most of the windows are still there and the doors have remained shut. No vandals around here,' he said with some satisfaction. 'Unlike Wellington,' he added quickly.

The inside had been spared the forces of nature over the years. Although securely shut the front door was unlocked, but it protested noisily when pushed open on hinges in need of some oil. Inside there was the type of mustiness they expected, and a good airing would address that problem. No furniture, other than a substantial old couch with hefty arm rests, and tufts of stuffing showing in places.

'Probably a fashionable piece once. Something a family used to sit on in front of a fire, maybe. Something that was once comfy to snuggle up on.'

There were a few minor holes in the internal walls, but that was just wear and tear. There was no evidence of malicious damage. The interior paint was well-worn, indicating a house that could be easily done up, and perhaps just the project they were looking for. The couple stood at the back door, picking out the faint outline of where a path had once been and the remains of a dog kennel.

'Come and look at this,' came the call. The kids were already investigating something interesting.

Both adults moved down the path following squeals of delight and laughter.

'Have you ever seen so much wasted fruit?' cried one of the children, who then picked up an armful of apples from a single tree and ran pelting the others with his supply. A vegetable patch was evident in the corner with a fence of sorts. Blackberry had all but destroyed it. Old plum trees and more piles of rotting fruit completed the picture. Rambling foliage covered a few derelict outbuildings and came right up to the house in places. It was not hard to imagine the property in its heyday, and what it could look like again if freshened with a coat of paint. It could be cleaned up over three or four weekends, and the couple stood envisaging freshly-finished walls and a well-tended garden. It was easy to picture previous decades. To almost hear the ring of happy voices from contented families who had once called this 'home'.

'It'll need work to get it back to the way it was,' she said, 'but I'm willing if you are.' There was a note of enthusiasm in the challenge.

At the gate the couple paused and looked back. It had that something they had been looking for, so there and then it was agreed they would make an offer. Dappled light shining through the orchard trees and the potential warmth of the place had helped cast aside any reservations.

'I bet,' he said, turning for the car, 'that this was once a really nice place to have been a kid.'

Backing down the driveway, the adults stopped at the road and waited for their children to catch them. They checked, but as expected found no other traffic and turned the car towards the real estate office in town.

• • • • • • •

Sun-bleached walls of the small wooden structure out beyond the house leaned at a crazy angle, with the whole thing semi-crushed under a weight of tangled vines. Plum trees, front and rear, barely supported but prevented its collapse, and rusty hinges just kept the door in place. It was slightly ajar, letting in a shaft of light to an interior that smelled of dampness and decay. With wooden boards having long rotted away, only dirt remained as a floor, and the earthy odour contributed to the shed's overall lack of appeal. Excited voices disturbed the occupant who now moved stealthily from his dark corner to investigate the commotion. In the gloom there was no telling how old the unsteady hands were that gripped the doorframe. They shook in anticipation, or was it more a tremor of apprehension? Narrowing the gap to minimise any chance of detection, and with an eye pressed to the crack, he watched children running and laughing. Watched quietly as the vehicle slowed to allow them to catch up. Satisfied they were only casual visitors, the man lurking in the Weta Shed began to pace back and forth. His confidence returned when he felt the hard shape of a knife in his pocket. He listened to slamming car doors, then returned to his spot in the corner. Settling back, he resumed his silent wait and muttered a few words from many years back, 'It's easier being the hunter than the hunted'.

They took it slowly on the way back, down a road not too narrow or windy, but one which encouraged a gentle ride. The new sealed surface was good, but even so they were in no real hurry. They simply wanted to enjoy the rural scene, and make sure the whole area had the right feel. Both adults were pretty well convinced the place they had seen was the answer to their dreams.

'I know she almost insisted we consider a beach bach on the west coast, but your Mum will absolutely love visiting this,' she said as the car crept towards, then stopped on a little bridge. 'She's probably never been over this side of the range. Probably never even lived in the country. The scene off to the left was picturesque, with the sound of gurgling water adding to the tranquility.

'I'm one hundred percent convinced she'll just adore our new country cottage, and I can't wait to bring her over here. It'll be a lovely surprise for her.'

'Who are you talking about?' came a child's tired but enquiring voice from the back seat.

'Your granny, dear.' The mother paused before adding, 'You know, Grandma from Palmerston North.'

POSTSCRIPT

Combined efforts from family and friends saw an immediate transformation of the old dwelling. In time, their attention turned to the rear garden area and what was left of various out-buildings. One particular shed was too far gone, and when the structure was eventually pulled down, decaying boards burst open to reveal colonies of hibernating wetas amongst dust and powdered rot. The ground crawled with a mass of barbed legs, fat, yellow and black bodies of all shapes and sizes, and angry, twitching feelers. While the odd weta scurried off to safety, others lay still, trying to remain camouflaged amongst the debris.

With the passing of that initial horror, and with old planks sporting rusted nails pulled well clear, the children jumped in, stamping as many of the hated creatures as they could find into a squashed pulp. Finally the area was raked clear of all material, leaving a solid earth floor which showed some sign of having been disturbed in recent years. A distinct slump in the dirt surface was dismissed as being a probable rubbish pit from some time back, and with the ground firm enough for their immediate needs, a fresh concrete pad was laid. The finished job left no evidence of the shed's previous existence, and with a pathway now linking the back-porch with this new slab, there would be no further slopping through wet grass to get to the clothesline.

'Grandma from Palmerston North' was never to see the rural property her eldest son and his family had bought. It was a cruel turn of events and she had felt a chill descend upon her when they had first described it. Those worst fears were confirmed some months later when photos were passed around showing the family's renovation efforts to date. Kitty's world appeared to be falling apart, and her state of mind was not helped by Bill's long absence these past months. Although only fifty years of age, the following months recorded a quiet decline in her general well-being as disturbing memories she thought had been well and truly put to rest years ago tormented her daily.

It was intended to be a quiet funeral. At the cemetery a small group of family and friends huddled together to say their farewells. Beyond the graveside, others who had known Kitty stood silently in ones and twos, respecting a family's unstated but obvious wish for private moments alone. Many faces were familiar to one another, but there were a few unknown ones too. During Kitty's life, she had touched the hearts of many. Although it had been over a year since her brother had last been in touch with loved ones, his absence today was out of character and frantic efforts earlier to track him down had proved fruitless. In time he would have some explaining to do to both employer and family.

Slowly the crowd disbursed, leaving a few stragglers and then eventually only one. He watched from afar as the last of the earth was filled in, flowers were rearranged, and then once workers had moved on, he made his way slowly through the rows of headstones. The eighty year old stepped up to the graveside and stared long and hard. He fingered a knife in his pocket acquired a year ago, to replace a flimsy modern one hurriedly purchased late one night at a dairy. This one was of more robust construction, and its weight suited him better. He had had no qualms about battering and burying its previous owner. The worn, but still evident skull emblems appealed to him, but above all Dwyer regarded it as being a trophy signifying the successful outcome of a long chase.

'Been a bit of a hunt, hasn't it, eh Kitty? One way or another, I'm finally rid of both of you.'